A Christmas To Remember

Kay Stockham

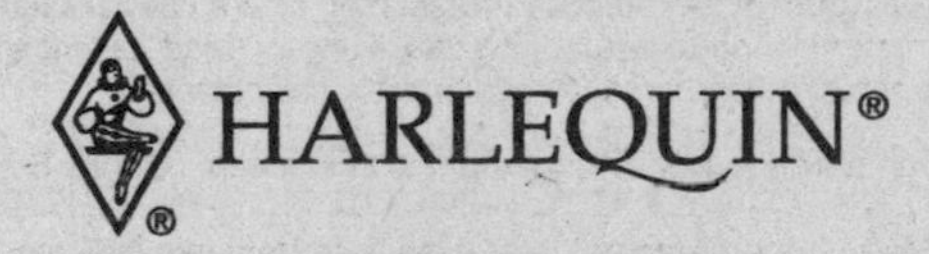

TORONTO • NEW YORK • LONDON
AMSTERDAM • PARIS • SYDNEY • HAMBURG
STOCKHOLM • ATHENS • TOKYO • MILAN • MADRID
PRAGUE • WARSAW • BUDAPEST • AUCKLAND

ISBN-13: 978-0-373-71453-7
ISBN-10: 0-373-71453-X

A CHRISTMAS TO REMEMBER

This edition published by arrangement with Harlequin Books S.A.

www.eHarlequin.com

Printed in U.S.A.

Marley stared into Beau's eyes, her mind filled with images she never wanted to revisit. Why her? Why now?

"It's not an act. I don't remember you." Beau's expression was one of concern, and despite the anger inside her, she felt drawn to him on a basic level. How sick and twisted was that?

She blinked hard to ease the sting of unwanted and humiliating tears. Beau moved yet closer, and she looked away. She didn't want him to scc what he could do to her after all this time.

A wicked scab covered a cut stretching from forehead to temple. The imperfections didn't detract from his looks, however. Beau was still tall, dark and horrible for a woman's equilibrium. *Pull yourself together.*

"Look, ah..." He lifted his arm, the one hanging in the sling. "I was in an accident and don't remember you. It's nothing personal. Maybe if you tell me your name?"

"No need. You've forgotten it–let's just leave it that way, shall we?" She wasn't sure how she managed to get the words out, but she did. With one last look at Beau, Marley retraced her steps to the garden she'd left.

It wasn't the greatest of exits. But given the way her legs shook, she figured getting back without falling on her face would have to do.

Dear Reader,

When I wrote *Man with a Past,* I knew Melissa would get her own story. She had to because she deserved a happy ending so badly. But what I wasn't expecting was all the e-mails and letters from you concerning Joe's kid brother. What happened to him? Where did he go? For a long, long time after the release, I received at least an e-mail a day. Great for a writer, bad for my muse. I didn't *know* what happened to him, and I didn't have a story.

I often pull my story ideas from music and the news, and during this time two things happened. A horrible tragedy took place and it was unthinkable what the families went through. I watched day after day to hear the updates on the people involved. The other event was the release of Nickelback's song titled "Photograph." I couldn't get either of these out of my mind. Eventually the two merged and I wondered what would happen if… And so this story was born.

I love the holidays, Christmas most of all, and hope *A Christmas To Remember* is worth the wait. I'd love to know what you think of this story. Write to me at P.O. Box 232, Minford, Ohio, 45653, or e-mail me at kay@kaystockham.com. And if you'd like information on me or my books, contests, newsletters and more, please visit my Web site at www.kaystockham.com.

God bless,

Kay

ABOUT THE AUTHOR

Kay Stockham has always wanted to be a writer, ever since she copied the pictures out of a Charlie Brown book and rewrote the story because she didn't like the plot. Formerly a secretary/office manager for a large commercial real estate development company, she's now a full-time writer and stay-at-home mom who firmly believes being a mom/wife/homemaker is the hardest job of all. Happily married for fifteen years and the somewhat frazzled mother of two, she's sold four books to Harlequin Superromance. Her first release, *Montana Secrets,* hit the Waldenbooks bestseller list and was chosen as a Holt Medallion finalist for Best First Book. Kay has garnered praise from reviewers for her emotional, heart-wrenching stories and looks forward to a long career writing a genre she loves.

Books by Kay Stockham

HARLEQUIN SUPERROMANCE

1307–MONTANA SECRETS
1347–MAN WITH A PAST
1395–MONTANA SKIES
1424–HIS PERFECT WOMAN

To Laura Shin for making me dig deep to find the story magic. I look forward to working with you on many stories to come!

To Dr. Cynthia Lea Clark, Psy.D., for responding to many, many e-mails. Any variation from protocol and timing was done for story purposes. Thank you!

To Bob Hurley, Custom Landscapes, for supplying all the seasonal planting advice–and to Sherri, his wife, for being my "Angel" for a lot of years.

To Suzanne Cox and Amy Knupp for riding this crazy ride with me. Your e-mails mean the world. Thanks for being such great friends and writers. And to the Pink Ladies at www.PinkLadiesBlog.com, we make a GREAT team.

And last but not least, to my family. Just for being you. I love you.

Merry Christmas!

CHAPTER ONE

HE BATTLED HIS WAY through the bands of fog that tried to drag him back into the darkness. He wanted to wake up, wanted to move, but his body was uncooperative.

Pain registered in varying degrees. His leg, his shoulder. His head. God help him, his head. It pounded in sync with his heartbeat, every throb a stab into his retinas. He managed to drag the arm that didn't hurt up to grasp and pull at the thing covering his face.

The oxygen mask snapped back when he lost his grip and the bump against his lower lip sent new pain through him. This woke him more fully, gave him the push needed to open his eyes.

He blinked, focused. Saw dingy walls, more gray than white, and a mud-colored water stain the size of a fist on the ceiling tile. Someone had tried painting over it, but the stain had seeped through.

Next came the steady beep of a machine somewhere above his head, another ticking noise behind him on his right. Two seconds later he heard a *click,* and the band around his upper arm tightened just shy of squeezing it in two.

A hospital. But why?

He heard a nasally, rumbling noise and turned his head to find the source. An older man sat in a chair beside the bed, slumped forward on the blanket covering him and snoring loud enough to wake the dead.

He grimaced at the effort it took to slide his hand down to where the man lay, but before he reached the guy's arm, his fingers encountered something hard. Head throbbing, he grasped the item and dragged it up until he could see what it was. A picture?

The two men in the photo smiled. They had similar looks despite the differences in age. Both held hunting rifles and wore camouflage. Written across their chests in loopy, feminine handwriting was "Barry & Beau, Thanksgiving 2002."

Blinking, he took in the room again, noticing a mirror attached to the door closest to the bed. He stared at himself a long moment, then looked back at the photograph. Same face. A little older, a lot rougher in appearance with all the stitches and swelling and bandages, but definitely the same.

The man in the chair snuffled out a loud, throat-blasting snore. The guy choked, coughed and woke. He raised his head and rubbed his eyes and—midyawn—glanced up and froze. Eyes flaring, he shot to his feet, the chair hitting the wall. "You're awake. You're *awake!*"

Was he? He wasn't so sure. Everything felt…off. Dreamlike. His mind was stuffed with cotton and his face unfamiliar except for the fact it was on the photograph he still held.

What was going on?

"Don't move," the man ordered, grinning as he hurried toward the door. "Don't move," he repeated over his shoulder before yanking the door open to yell, "Doc? *Doc!* He's awake, come quick!"

Running footsteps thundered toward the room, growing louder as they grew close. A man in a white lab coat burst into the room.

"Glad to see you're back, soldier. My name is Major Abrams, and I'm your doctor. Let me check you over and then we'll get down to business."

Before he could find his voice, the physician pulled a minilight from his pocket and blinded him with it, ordering him to keep his eyes open despite the daggers of pain stabbing his brain. A couple of torturous seconds later, the doc straightened and wrote down some notes on his chart.

"What happened?" He sounded like a frog after a dry spell.

"What's the last thing you remember?"

He searched for an answer, but didn't find one.

"It's okay, take your time and wake up a bit. Are you seeing double?"

"No."

"How many fingers am I holding up?"

"Three. Where am I?"

"You're in Landshuhl Army Hospital." The doctor pointed to a whiteboard across the room. "What's written on the board over there?"

The pain in his head and the brightness of the lights left him squinting. "Your nurse today is Lt. Pauley."

"Very good." The doctor pulled out a stethoscope and pressed it to his chest. "What's my name again?"

He frowned. "Major Abrams."

"Good. And your lungs are clear, which is excellent. Now, back to the original question. Can you tell us what happened?"

He frowned, struggling, his thoughts too fast to catch, a speeding blur he couldn't focus on or stop. "I'm not sure."

"That's fine," the doctor murmured, continuing his exam. "After a head injury like yours, it's perfectly normal to be a little confused. Don't be alarmed. It would be unusual if you did remember details. That's why I'm grilling you with these questions."

"Do you know what happened?" He hated having to ask. Hated the nothingness where the answers should've been.

He stared at the older man who'd been sleeping beside his bed, then did his best to ignore the expression on the guy's face, the one that said whatever had landed him in the hospital hadn't been good.

"Son—"

"The details can wait," the doctor stated firmly, his gaze brooking no argument from the other man. "After we get some tests out of the way."

His heart rate increased, the beeps on the machine behind him sounding closer together. Awareness slid into his consciousness in place of his memories. Something was wrong, something big.

"Tell me what's going on." His gaze locked on

the older man and refused to let him look away. "Who are you?"

The guy paled, becoming the same gray as the walls.

Abrams cleared his throat. "Let's take this one step at a time, soldier."

Terror gathered inside him, a rolling, building wave growing higher and wider with every second that passed. "I want to know now. Tell me what's going on." The doctor murmured something about tests again and he cursed. "*Tell* me!"

The older man staggered to the other side of the small room. The man shook, and that sight had his hand tightening into a fist. The plastic picture frame bent, the edge sharp against his skin.

He'd remember everything in a minute. It was the pressure. Had to be. He'd just woken up. It was— *The picture.* "He's Barry."

The man turned, his expression hopeful, a relieved smile forming on his lips.

The right answer, but why didn't the name mean anything? Barry. *Barry?* The knowledge, the memory, wasn't there. And he could tell by the way the doctor watched him that he knew it. He wasn't fooling anyone.

He tried to swallow the lump in his throat. "I'm Beau." He held on to the picture so tightly he heard his knuckle pop. "I'm *Beau.*" The monitor behind him filled the room with ever increasing bleeps.

"You're Beau," Major Abrams agreed with a slow nod. "But?"

He fought back humiliating tears as the roar of

waves crashed over him, dragging him under. From a distance, he heard someone shouting.

Dizzy, sick, he raised his hand to his head, tried to ease the ache. He hit his face instead, the plastic frame scratching him. The harder he tried to remember, the worse the pain became, slicing through his skull until it was impossible to think, to concentrate.

"Why can't I remember?" He dropped the picture and grabbed the man by his lab coat, needing something to anchor him, to hold him together. "*Why can't I remember?*"

The doctor's mouth moved, but he couldn't understand the words. Cold wetness touched him and a needle pricked his arm. Seconds later a peacefulness settled over him.

Everything began to blur. Fog crept in again until he was surrounded by darkness, lost and floating. Adrift.

"AMNESIA?" SIX HOURS LATER, Barry Buchanan paced Major Abrams's office floor, his inhaler clutched in his hand. He'd had to puff on the thing off and on all day to combat the wheezing and stress.

After watching his son lose it in full-blown panic, he shook like a compacting machine. Six hours and he still couldn't get the sound of Beau's hoarse shouts out of his head. He'd felt every ounce of his son's gut-clenching fear, and couldn't imagine how terrifying it would be to wake up and not know his own name. Now Beau was worn-out and much too quiet.

"How can this happen? This is…this is something

off a *soap opera.*" Barry stalked to the window and kept his back to the doc, afraid the Major might see how close he was to losing it himself.

Four days ago he'd gotten the call that Beau had been injured and was being transported from Iraq to Germany. He'd dropped everything, hopped a flight with nothing more than a couple changes of clothes in a backpack and hadn't had more than a few hours of sleep since. He'd waited by Beau's bedside, praying. Begging God for Beau to wake up, to be okay. But now that he had— "How can he not remember *anything?*"

"I know this is a shocking turn of events, but it's not uncommon to experience memory loss after the kind of head trauma your son sustained. With time he'll be able to adjust and most of his memories should return."

"How can you or anyone else expect that boy to *adjust* to not remembering who he is?"

The doctor ran a hand over his hair, the high-and-tight military cut leaving him nearly bald. "The road ahead will be difficult, but he will. The technical term for his condition is *retrograde amnesia.* Depending on the trauma sustained by the patient, the length of the memory loss may vary. In your son's case, it's severe. At least in regard to certain things."

"Certain things? He doesn't remember half his life! He doesn't remember his own father!"

"No, he doesn't," the doctor agreed calmly. "But Beau has retained his education. He knows how to read, count. His short-term memory is unaffected, his vision is fine and there are no signs of hemorrhages in his skull. All of which add up to a very good prognosis."

"When will he get his memory back?"

"That's something I can't answer. Patients recover at their own rate, Mr. Buchanan. Your son's memory could return before we go back to his room to talk to him—or it could be weeks or even months. The worst-case scenario is that he never regains his memories, *but* that is the worst case. Given time, the odds are well in his favor that he'll regain his memory of everything except the time around which the actual injury occurred, and that is perfectly normal. We need to focus on the positives right now, and not the aspects out of our control."

"What's the longest anyone's ever gone before their memory returned?"

The doc looked distinctly uncomfortable. "There have been case studies lasting as long as twenty-four months."

"Two *years?*" How did someone function for two years without their memories?

"That's not the norm," Major Abrams stressed. "But there are no hard-and-fast rules where the brain is concerned." He shifted in his chair. "Mr. Buchanan, I'll arrange to have one of our mental-health professionals talk to you as soon as possible about what you can do to help your son, but the fact is it's all a waiting game. Pushing or rushing your son to remember before he's ready will not help him and could actually cause more damage. Regaining his memories or talking to him about them is a process. A slow one that needs to be performed by a professional."

Barry paced, too frustrated to sit down and have the discussion in a calm, straightforward manner.

"The good news here is that your son not only survived, he's young and healthy and the shrapnel injuries are healing quickly. There's no reason why he shouldn't make a full recovery. It's just going to take some time and patience."

Barry rubbed his gritty eyes and exhaled roughly. "But we still have to go back into that room and tell him he's not going to remember any time soon."

The doctor's gaze slipped down to the inhaler Barry held in his hand, then back up to his face. "I can do that myself if you'd rather not be present."

He shook his head, knowing no matter how tired or worn-out he was, he couldn't let his son face this alone. "No. Beau might not remember me, but I'm still his father. I'll stay by his side…no matter what. That poor boy who died, Beau's buddy— His father turned his back on him when he needed him most. I won't do that to my son. I won't do that to Beau."

CHAPTER TWO

MARLEY ENTERED her parents' house and listened intently. How could anyone be *that* quiet?

"Mama, you home?" She walked through the foyer and into the kitchen, carrying the miniature sunflower she'd bought at the nursery.

It had been a successful trip, not as expensive as she'd thought it would be, so she hummed as she searched the cabinets for a plastic plate to go underneath the pot. She found what she needed in her mother's old entertaining stash gathering dust in the pantry. At the sink, a quick flip of the tap watered the dry soil.

Marley smiled down at the bright flower, amazed how something so simple could cheer her up on just about any given day. There was something about growing things, nurturing them from seeds and watching them blossom into something beautiful.

Please let her like it.

"What are you doing?"

At the edge she heard in the softly spoken query Marley froze, then pasted a smile back on her lips before turning to face her mother. She was still in her housecoat, the burgundy and black colors fading her already pale complexion to ghostlike extremes. At forty-five, Donna Pierce appeared older, the lines and grooves around her mouth and eyes telling a traumatic story.

"I, um, dropped by to bring you this." She forced into her tone a cheeriness she didn't feel. "Isn't it beautiful? I thought you'd like the reds and oranges, and the pot matches the kitchen. Can't beat that, right?"

Her mother didn't move, much less look at the pot. "It's very nice, Marley, but you shouldn't have bothered."

"Oh, it was no bother. I thought you'd like it so I—"

"You know how forgetful I am these days. It won't get watered properly and then you'll have wasted your money."

So much for being appreciative. Strained, Marley glanced around the immaculate kitchen and noted that the housekeeper had come recently to clean. "Um… Have you eaten lunch? I thought we could—"

"Roberta is dropping by soon," her mother said with a glance at her watch. "I need to get dressed and… She said we have a lot to talk about."

"Oh. Well, maybe I could get lunch and bring it back for u—" She broke off when she spied the look of utter panic flickering across her mother's face. "I guess not." Marley wet her dry lips. "Mama, are you ever going to feel comfortable having me around your friends again?"

Her mother wrung her hands. "I don't know what you mean. If you want to stay, Marley, stay."

Now, that was a warm invitation. Marley shook

her head, an attempt to fend off the hurt threatening her. Dwelling on it only made it worse. "You know what, forget it. I've got a lot of work to do today and you don't see your friends that often. Just forget I asked."

Her mother padded over to the cabinet and after retrieving a glass, she poured herself some water. Her hands trembled as she pulled a small, brown bottle from her pocket and shook out a tiny white pill.

Marley stepped closer, watching her. "Are you sick?"

"No. It's just—it's just something Dr. Bourke gave me to calm my nerves when…when I get upset."

Like when I'm around? Marley fisted her hands and refused to give in to the tears stinging her eyes. She had to stop reading things into her mother's comments, but how could she not after "the incident"? "Dr. Myners was your doctor for years. Why did you switch?"

Casual conversation was good. They needed to stick with it. Build a bridge over the past since they couldn't seem to wade through it no matter how hard she tried to make up for embarrassing her mother with a teenage pregnancy.

"I still see him." Her mother placed the pill on her tongue with the delicateness of a Duchess at tea and swallowed, taking a drink before setting the cup aside.

Desperate, Marley stepped forward and wrapped her arms around her mom, but the moment she did she felt the tension, the awkwardness, and her hopes fell as they always did. Five years and counting and her mother still hadn't forgiven her. "I love you, Ma."

A brisk pat on her back was her answer. "I love you, too."

Perfunctory. Her mother's response was perfunctory, the response one made when someone said those three words and a comment was warranted. Maybe her mother did love her still, but if that were the case, it was conditional love, and Marley's appalling fall from grace had made it that. The wild child too much for her mother's ultraconservative ways. That they were such total polar opposites didn't seem possible, but it was true.

"I'm glad you're okay," she murmured, her voice thicker than she wanted. "I—I'm going to go now."

"Do you need something before you leave? A drink to take with you? Perhaps you'd like to take the plant? I don't mind."

Marley retreated the way she always did, too afraid to risk upsetting her mother's fragile mental state. Terrified of being the cause of another breakdown. "No, Ma, nothing. Thanks. And you keep the plant. I—if you forget to water it, it's okay. Enjoy it while it lasts."

"Well, if you're sure." An awkward silence stretched between them, broken only by the sound of the grandfather clock chiming in the hall. "Your father says you're staying busy. You go back to work and have a good day."

Smiling weakly, Marley put her feet into motion. "I am… I will. I'll just…go."

Her mother sighed in obvious relief, seeming old despite having the bone structure and figure of a much younger woman.

"That's probably best. I'm feeling a bit tired now. I think I'll call Roberta and tell her to come another day."

"But you have lots to talk about, you said so." Surely she wasn't such a chore to be around that her mother would cancel her plans after five minutes?

Marley paused. Did her mother look a bit dazed? She'd only just taken the medicine and no pill worked that quickly. Had she taken something earlier?

"I know what I said, Marley, but I'm not up to company now."

"Would you like me to—"

"No. I'll be fine. You just go do what you have to do. I like the quiet of the house. It soothes me."

Hurt even though she knew she should be used to getting the brush-off from her mother, Marley left the kitchen via the back door because it was the closest. She stomped her way down the steps. "So much for hoping the flower would cheer her up. She likes the *quiet.* Do I talk too much? Get on her nerves?" The image of her mother popping that pill came to mind, and she shook her head again. There was her answer.

The walk around the large brick house should have been a beautiful one, but the once-immaculate flower beds were filled with overgrown weeds, the award-winning herb garden long gone. The fruit trees needed trimming and her childhood playhouse turned potting shed needed a new coat of paint.

At one time she and her mother would've done all of those things together, spending too many hours to count side by side on their knees in the dirt. But not now. Maybe never again since her mother treated her like one of *those* family members—the kind who wasn't discussed in front of friends.

Five years was a long time to hold a grudge. *And yet her mother did.*

Marley followed the stone path to the garden gate and left, every step she took angrier than the last because her mom wouldn't return her hug and had barely acknowledged the sunflower she'd paid way too much for.

Why had she bothered? She couldn't change the past or the hurt she'd caused, and sometimes she was sick of trying when her mother never gave an inch. She relied on others for her self-worth. How could anyone fight that?

Yanking open the door to her truck, Marley climbed in and sat in the September sun before starting the engine.

Time to trudge on and pretend she didn't care.

TWO WEEKS AFTER waking up in the hospital, Beau Buchanan squinted against the noonday sun scorching the housing development going up outside South Ridge, Kentucky, and eyed the woman talking to the development's manager.

The woman's hands lifted and lowered in expressive gestures, a frown deeply etched on her face. The sun made her red hair shine all red and gold and molten at once. The thick mass was scraped into a ponytail two inches thick, which hung down her back in corkscrew spirals that bounced and danced with every gesture she made. He smiled, dumbstruck by her glorious hair. Would it feel as soft as it looked?

Whoa, boy, you're not up for that yet.

Maybe not, but the thought brought a curiosity all its own. Beau shook his head and limped over to the truck like a three-legged dog. It would be a long time before he was ready for a hookup. Some things took priority and getting his memory back was top of the list. Besides, no woman in her right mind would want to deal with his in the state it was in.

He glanced over at the woman again, noticing the heat and humidity had her red curls fighting for freedom around her face. It looked as though they were winning the battle, too. She kept raising a hand to brush away the strands sticking to her forehead and temples in straggly ringlets, attempting to tuck them into the confining band. Doing so only seemed to free more.

He smothered a laugh when he spied the dark smudges left by her grimy hands. She was filthy. And adorable. About five and a half feet and a pretty sight, dirt and all. She wore faded jeans that cradled her slim hips to perfection, and a hot pink T-shirt with a big tree on the front.

"Not bad, huh?"

The rank smell of unwashed teenager reached him seconds before the boy. The kid was young, raw, and his shirt had the same logo as the woman's, which he now saw said, Marley's Treehouse, Landscaping & Garden Center. Instead of pink, however, the kid's once-blue shirt was now a sweat-and-grime-smeared brown.

Beau nodded in the woman's direction. "Not bad at all. She your boss?"

"Yeah. But you might as well stop staring. The only thing she's interested in is getting the first two houses planted before the fall and Christmas rush hits."

"It's a long time till Christmas."

"Not when you've got other contracts to get done, and people are screwing up here. No offense, you're part of the electrical team, right?"

Beau nodded. "What happened?"

The kid flicked a glob of mud off his chest. "The painters tossed their crap outside to pick up later."

"But they didn't do it," he murmured, having watched the woman and kid cleaning up the debris for the last hour or so.

"Nope. And it's put us behind. She's ticked about it because it's the second time it's happened. Said she was going to talk to the site manager to make sure it's not held against her."

It shouldn't be. Some of the subcontractors were worse than others about cleanup, and he could certainly see where she'd be upset since she couldn't work until the area was clear. "She the only female sub here?"

The kid smirked. "Yeah. Some of the guys are pissed, too, because the developer chose her over one of the big dogs in town. I think they're hoping she'll quit."

Beau winced. She was in a tight spot. If she let any of them get by with leaving their trash, she'd be cleaning it up the entire length of the contract, but if she complained too much, she could come across as incompetent and bitchy.

"Hey, think I could have a bottle of water?" The kid indicated the cooler with a grubby hand.

Beau opened the lid, willing to part with the precious commodity in exchange for information on the first thing to take his mind off his amnesia since he woke up in the hospital. "Sure…enjoy."

"Thanks. Hey, I'm Eli."

"Beau."

"Hey," the kid said again, lifting the bottle in greeting. "So what happened to you?"

Beau glanced down at the sling on his right arm and the thick bandage wrapped around his left thigh above the knee. "Shrapnel."

"No kidding? You were shot?"

He shrugged. "Something like that."

"Cool. You a cop or something?"

"Ex-Marine," he murmured, really wanting a change of subject. *Cool?*

The boy took a long draw from the bottle then wiped his mouth, leaving a muddy streak behind. He focused on what was taking place across the street, and Beau followed the kid's gaze. The man she'd been talking to now nodded in agreement to whatever she was saying.

"Gotta give it to her, man, she's good. She gets her way every time."

"He gets his way every time just because he's smaller!"

CHAPTER THREE

THE WORDS SLAMMED into Beau's brain accompanied by a jagged pain and an image. A bedroom, a cluttered desk, a model airplane lying broken on the floor.

It was no more than a quick flash, but his already aching head felt as if it would explode as a result.

He braced his hand on the truck for balance, unable to believe that after his visits to the shrink in Germany and then the introductory one here with no success, he'd finally remembered something and all because of what the kid had said.

"Hey, dude, you okay?"

He nodded carefully, searching his mind to try to identify the voice. Was it his? Someone else's? It had belonged to someone young, boyish.

"Maybe you should drink some water."

"No, I'm okay. I'm good."

The teen snorted. "If you say so. Look, take it easy. I've gotta get back to work 'cause I'm only here half a day, but yell if you need help, okay?"

"Yeah. See you later." Beau lifted his hand in a weak wave as the kid walked away with a confident strut.

Maybe Pop was right. Maybe it was too soon to

come to work, but the walls had been closing in on him at the rental house Pop had found for them. The job site was a good hundred fifty miles from their Cincinnati home, and Pop hadn't wanted to leave him behind to recover with him working so far away.

Shaking his head, Beau turned his attention to the wire he'd come to retrieve from the rear of the truck. He leaned his weight against the frame and pretended the gravel beneath his feet wasn't moving. Ignoring the sensation as best he could, he lifted the large roll with his uninjured arm and tensed when the few remaining stitches pulled. The sling would be off by the end of the week, but Pop would throw a fit if he saw him carrying anything heavier than a gallon of milk.

Back under the shaded eave, he squinted over his shoulder to see the woman back at work in the yard opposite the house where Buchanan & Son Specialty Electric worked. She was on her knees, digging in the dirt beneath the window of the first home listed for sale by the housing developer.

Straightening, she put her hands at the base of her back and pressed as though to stretch out a kink. Once again an image flashed through his mind, that of another woman kneeling over something. Laughter and paper and red. Lots of red...paint?

"Come on, sweetheart. We've got to get these signs painted before the Pee Wee game starts. You don't want to be late, do you?"

"You okay, son?"

Pop's question jerked him out of his daze and the image skittered away like the leaves in the wind. "Just a headache." He didn't want to get his father's hopes up that his memory was coming back when there was so much he didn't know or recognize. Who was the kid? The woman?

"How long have you had this one?"

He looked over at Pop and smiled wearily. "I'm fine, quit worrying. You know her?" He nodded toward the woman and hoped the change in subject would get Pop to lay off.

His dad pulled the ball cap from his head and scratched what was left of his hair. "She's the landscaper. Heard some of the men have been giving her a hard time. Why? She say something to you?"

"No." He relayed what the kid had said. "I saw her talking to the site manager a minute ago."

"I'll talk to the boys about it. Dean's usually the worst about leaving his trash behind, but I won't put up with any nonsense. Shame people just can't get along." His gaze narrowed. "You know, you can't hide the pain on your face."

"It's fine. But I think I'm about ready to go home if you or one of the guys are going to make a run for lunch."

"That bad, huh? Come on, I'll give the boys their orders and we'll get out of here. You get too hot? You've been puttering around here all morning. You might have heatstroke. It's muggy for September."

"It's just a headache," he repeated. "Besides, it's cooler out here than it is cooped up in there."

Pop looked skeptical, but nodded anyway. "True enough. Still, maybe it's time to set up another appointment to have that hard head of yours looked at.

Maybe go talk to the shrink again? Doc Abrams said some patients go to sessions three times a week."

Once a week was more than enough for him. After the appointments overseas, Pop had been fine with his decision to take things as they came because the sessions frustrated him so much, but he knew why Pop now pushed to up his visits. After his behavior this morning, all the guys were sending him leery looks.

Rationally, he knew it was wise of them to keep a close watch on him given his military training, but it didn't make being the object of such scrutiny any more tolerable. Who wanted to be thought of as a few too many puzzle pieces short?

"I just didn't want to go inside." He hated that Pop saw him acting so strange, much less the crew.

His father had bid on the large housing project over a year ago and started work a month or so before getting the call that he'd been injured. Pop had checked in daily while he was away, but they were running behind.

The last thing his father needed now was to be distracted by his behavior on top of the memory thing.

"Any particular reason why? Did you remember something?"

Jaw tight, Beau shook his head in response to the question. He couldn't explain it. The tightness in his chest, the way every nerve in his body felt on edge the moment he stepped through the doorway into the unfinished interior. The guys laughing, joking, the radio blaring. There was a familiarity to it, a sense of doom, too. If only he could remember why.

"Well, don't worry about it. Given the choice, I'd much rather be outside, too."

Maybe, but if that was the case why was Pop giving him the look of concern that had been constant during his hospital vigil? "I'm fine," he insisted again. "Besides, being jumpy doesn't count as a breakthrough. I don't need to visit the shrink, what I need is to get back to work."

"Soon as you have an okay from your PT doc, you can."

Uh-huh. What would Pop's excuse be then? His father had been babying him ever since he'd woken up, trying to take care of him and work a business, too. Had Pop struggled to keep things running with him overseas and not lending a hand?

"Why'd I join up? Why did I leave you to do it all?" He indicated the truck door and the sign painted on the side. "It isn't Buchanan & Son for nothing, right?"

His father stared into his eyes for a long moment. Startled by the question? "No, it's not. But it was something you needed to do."

Beau narrowed his gaze. "What aren't you saying?"

After a deep breath, Pop made eye contact again. "I suppose it wouldn't hurt to tell you how things came about." He pulled his cap off and scratched his head again. "Beau…your joining up was ordered by the court. You had to choose between jail or the military."

"I've got a record?"

Pop nodded. "You've been in trouble a few times,

vandalism, petty stuff. You made a nuisance of yourself and irritated the judge, and he had this thing about giving his cases a choice when they didn't straighten up. When the order came down, you chose the military, but when your time was up and you could've come home, you chose to stay."

"Court-ordered?" That was a lot to take in. He couldn't imagine being that person. "How long ago was this?"

"You went before the judge about five years ago. You were in trouble off and on for three or four years before that."

Beau rubbed his forehead, trying to work through the new information. "Okay so...why did I stay in the military?"

"I can't answer that other than to say that after a while you liked it. You had some growing up to do and the military helped. Eventually you became something other than the numb-nut always getting into trouble for the heck of it."

Smiling at Pop's description, his gaze landed on the truck door and the Buchanan & Son sign, questions filling his head. If he asked too many, his father would clam up because the docs and shrink said it was better if he remembered on his own, but if he stuck to the general...

"Give me that wire and stop gabbing like an old woman so we can go get us some food."

"I can take it in." He planned to, too, except he got to the door and the sick feeling swept over him again, making him light-headed.

Pop squeezed his good arm. "Take it slow, and don't argue. You know you shouldn't be carrying that anyway. I'll take it to the guys while you go grab my cell out of the truck. I need to call about some equipment before we go."

Since he didn't think he could force himself through the entry, he released the wire. His father hefted the roll onto his shoulder while Beau retraced his steps to the truck to look for the phone. He pretty much collapsed into the grit-covered seat before beginning his search beneath the papers and empty coffee cups. What was the deal? What was it about going into the unfinished house that brought on the cold sweats? Something about the bomb? About what he'd been doing before the explosion?

"Awww, come on back, sweetie, I said I was sorry. I like watching you bend over to pick it up, but I'll get it."

Beau raised his head at Dean's words. The man held long wire scraps in his hands and faced the landscaper with an insincere leer Beau wanted to wipe off his face. Dean had been mouthing off all morning about this or that, and Beau was tired of the disrespect. He should probably keep his mouth shut and let his father handle the crew, but enough was enough. "Is there a problem?" he called from inside the truck.

His question drew the woman's attention. Their gazes locked, and like an idiot he smiled at her, hoping to smooth the waters. It didn't. In fact, she stumbled to a stop, her eyes widening in a mixture of shock and something else he couldn't identity. Through the windshield he watched as she paled, and for a minute he was afraid she'd actually pass out. Swooning at the sight of him?

In his dreams.

He frowned at her reaction, getting out as quickly as possible and trying not to favor his bum leg too much as he made his way to her. The sling was bad enough, his face a mess of scabs. Figures their first meeting would be one where she'd probably think he couldn't take care of himself.

"You... *You?*" she asked when he drew near. Her voice was hoarse, her chest rising and falling rapidly as she continued to stare at him, looking like a deer frozen in headlights.

"Me." He added another smile. "Do I know you?"

Expressions flickered over her face in rapid succession. Shock gave way to pain, hurt to anger. "Nice."

"Did I do something wrong?"

Bright green eyes stared into his, and the woman's hands fisted at her sides. "Seriously?" The word was barely a whisper. "You're *seriously* going to stand there and pretend you don't even—" Her voice broke and she cleared her throat determinedly. "Nice."

He stepped closer. "Look, obviously you know me, but you're going to have to give me a hint here, sweetheart."

Her jaw firmed at the endearment. "I am not your sweetheart."

And he got the feeling he'd stumbled into a minefield. Dean stood behind her, making no attempt to hide his appreciation as he studied her backside. Eli stood off to the side, a confused look on his face as if he didn't know whether to charge in swinging or stay out of the way. Smart kid chose the latter.

Beau took another step and she backed up before she caught herself and stood her ground. "Drop the act."

"Let me explain."

"Explain what?" A bitter sound came from her throat. "What are you doing here, Beau?"

CHAPTER FOUR

MARLEY STARED into Beau's beautiful blue eyes and despised the quivering sensation inside her, her mind filled with images she never wanted to revisit. Why her? Why *now?*

"It's not an act. I don't remember you." Beau's expression was one of concern and despite the anger that had built inside her over the past five years, she felt drawn to him on a basic level. How sick and twisted was that? The only person Beau had ever been concerned about was himself, and he'd proven it to her in the cruelest way.

Marley blinked hard to ease the sting of unwanted and humiliating tears. This was adding to the stress of her mother's coldness and the little hold she maintained on her self-control was rapidly slipping. In response Beau moved yet closer, his gaze locked on hers. She looked away. She didn't want him to see what he could do to her after all this time.

A scab covered a cut stretching from forehead to temple and it matched the other cuts and scrapes on his face, a few colorful bruises beginning to fade with purple and yellow hues. The imperfections didn't detract from his looks, however. Beau was still tall, dark and horrible for a woman's equilibrium.

Pull yourself together. Trying to do just that, she took in the width of his chest, and noted the arm not covered by a royal blue sling was corded with muscle.

"Are you okay?"

Not exactly. She nodded, unable to speak because of the lump of fear lodged in her throat. Despite the numerous times she'd held this very confrontation in her head, she was speechless. Amazing.

"Look, ah…" He lifted his arm, the one hanging in the sling. "I was in an accident and don't remember so well these days."

She snorted, wondering how many women had bought that story when he told it. "It's okay, Beau. Spare me the lies and the games. There isn't any need for them and I heard plenty from you five years ago."

Beau closed what little distance remained between them and she stiffened. Heat rolled off him, hotter than the sun overhead. A frown pulled his brows into a deep V, and she had to give him credit, he really did look confused. For a second her resolve faltered, but no. Lying came as second nature to him.

"It's not a lie. Crazy as it sounds, I have amnesia."

Marley blinked then released a ragged laugh. "I see," she drawled, unable to control her sarcasm but careful to keep her voice low due to their audience. She shook her head, disgusted with herself and him.

Who was he trying to kid? Beau had been well-known among his friends as being a BS'er. But *amnesia?* She'd read novels with better story lines.

"I'm not lying." He squeezed the cell phone so tight the belt clip unhinged from the casing with a *snap.* "I'm sorry I don't recognize you, but at least give me a chance to explain."

She shook her head firmly. "Save it." No way would he do this to her *again.*

"What did I—" He groaned and shut his eyes, lifting the hand that held the phone to his head and rubbing hard. "Look," he continued in a softer tone, "I was in the Marines and took a couple of hits, one of which was to my head. See the scar? I don't remember things now. I don't remember *you.* It's nothing personal."

Her mouth parted to draw in much-needed air. *Nothing personal?*

Beau squinted at her, and standing so close she saw the strain etched on his features. Beau might have been good when it came to putting on a show for potential bedmates, but she didn't think he could fake that much pain. She saw it now that the shock was starting to wear off.

"Maybe if you tell me your name?"

"No need. You've forgotten it, let's just leave it that way, shall we?"

She turned to go back to work, but Beau caught her arm in a gentle grip. "Wait."

"What's going on here?" An older man emerged from a house the crew was working on and hurried toward them. "Is there a problem?"

Beau dropped his hold, but not until he'd slid his hand down the length and left a trail of fire behind. Taking a couple steps back, he waited.

People watched. She could feel them, knew they were the topic of conversation all around the site as more and more of the workers paused to see what was happening.

More attention. Just what she didn't need. Why now? Why *now?* Marley fought the panic. She'd worked so hard to overcome her past, to make up with her family. How long would it be before the gossips informed her parents of Beau's presence in town? Here? "Beau was telling me a story." She struggled to find a careless smile and knew her effort came up lacking.

"It's not a 'story,'" Beau insisted again. "Pop, help me out here."

"I'm Barry Buchanan." Stepping close, the older man stuck out his hand and waited until she reluctantly placed her smaller palm in his. "Buchanan & Son Electric. You know my son?"

"We've met." She could certainly see the resemblance. Mr. Buchanan wore a ball cap, but he had the same intense blue eyes, the same build. Beau stood a good three inches above his father, but it was easy to picture the man Beau would become. Physically, anyway.

First impressions being what they were, Barry Buchanan seemed like a sincere man. A friendly, fatherly type. Too bad his son was a louse.

"You own the landscaping business, right? I heard about the trouble some of the men have been giving you. I want to assure you I won't put up with it from my crew. You let me know if they give you any problems."

She ignored the snort she heard behind her.

Barry Buchanan didn't. "Dean, why're you standing around like—" The man's gaze narrowed on the worker who'd been harassing her, then shifted to her. "Something happen?"

Dean was the least of her problems at the moment.

"I was just playing around," Dean said. "It won't happen again. Sorry, ma'am."

She nodded.

Mr. Buchanan sent the man back to work with a pointed glare, then shifted his attention to her. "I saw the mock-up of the plans. These houses will sell fast once you get things looking pretty. What was your name again?"

Beau's father was being so good ol' boy polite, Marley couldn't blast him with her anger. "Marley Pierce. I own Marley's Treehouse."

She saw Beau frown as though mulling over her name, and her anger increased. She knew guys thought differently, but did they really forget the women they played? How could he have forgotten getting her *pregnant?*

Because you didn't matter to him.

"Nice to meet you, Ms. Pierce. As for Beau, my son's telling you the truth. He's fresh from Iraq and sporting a few wounds as you can see. It's not a game that he can't remember you."

Unable to do anything but accept the man's words about his son, she nodded. "I see. Well, Beau, I'm sorry for what happened to you and…I'll let you both get back to work."

She wasn't sure how she managed to get the words out, but she did. With one last look at Beau, Marley turned on her heel and retraced her steps to the garden she'd left.

It wasn't the greatest of exits. In fact, it wasn't impressive at all, but given the way her legs shook she figured getting back to where she was supposed to be without falling on her face would have to do.

"THAT WAS...interesting." Pop waggled his fingers for Beau to hand him the phone. "Let me make that call and we'll go in a few minutes."

Beau nodded, but didn't take his gaze off Marley Pierce. She obviously couldn't wait to get away from him, but before leaving she'd hesitated and looked him dead in the eyes.

He'd hurt her and hurt her bad.

The pain on her face had shot straight to his gut and made him feel like the lowest of the low. It didn't take a genius to figure out sex had been part of whatever had happened. He couldn't imagine knowing Marley Pierce and not wanting her. Not when he wanted her now despite the pain of his injuries. Her mouth had looked soft and delicious, and her lips had quivered with the anger she felt toward him, but he'd noticed the goose bumps on her arms despite the heat. A strong response, one he wanted to explore. The fact that she'd known him before only made her more intriguing.

Amnesia. How many guys had used that line over the years as everything from a pickup to an excuse? Had he used it on her? Pretended not to remember?

He grimaced. She didn't know what to make of

his memory loss and neither did he. But he wanted answers Pop refused to give him, and Marley Pierce might be the key to getting them.

"Okay, let's go."

Beau climbed into the truck, unable to pull his gaze from her. "Do you know when I met her?"

Pop released a gusty sigh. "No, son, I don't. But I think it's apparent things didn't end well. You'd best keep away from her. You've got enough on your plate to deal with right now."

True enough. Beau tilted his head and winced when it felt as though someone was using his brain as a drum. He motioned to the house across the street and the woman shoveling dirt as if there was a pot of gold at the bottom of the hole. "She blasted me for being a liar. Come on, Pop, give me something. Do you know what happened with us? What I said to her?"

His father started the diesel engine. "I don't know what happened with that girl and even if I did, I couldn't tell you. The doc's said—"

"I have to remember on my own." He growled the words, disgusted with himself.

Pop rubbed his hand roughly over his face and let the truck idle. "Look, Beau, if it makes you feel any better, you had a lot of *friends* I knew nothing about. Girls looking for more when you were only looking for a good time. I'd say she was one of them. All I know is that I've got better things to do than to play ref between the two of you, and I'd better not see you giving her a hard time. I'm here for a job and running behind, and you need to recuperate. Hassling some girl isn't going to help either one of us. Leave that one alone, you hear me?"

Once again he glanced over at the house. Marley Pierce was rounded in all the right places, and memory or not, he liked what he saw. All except her expression.

"That's an order, Beau. I don't need some woman siccing the law on you for stalking. If she wants to talk to you, she will."

Pop's words rang true and he knew it. They didn't need that kind of trouble and Marley Pierce looked angry enough, hurt enough, to call in reinforcements if she felt they were necessary.

But if she'd known him five years ago she might be able to tell him where he'd liked to go and hang out. What he'd liked to do. Music, movies. Friends? Maybe talking with her would jar his memory. Give him something to go on rather than the big, fat nothing he had now.

His head throbbed in response to his thoughts and the vibration from the motor made him rub his temple in a useless effort to rid himself of the pain.

Marley kept her head carefully averted when they drove by her. He stared anyway, just in case she looked up, and he settled himself more comfortably in the seat, his mind made up. He'd talk to Marley later—after she'd had a chance to calm down and adjust to the fact she was going to be seeing him on a regular basis.

MARLEY NEARLY CHOPPED her toes off with the shovel.

Swearing beneath her breath, she waited impatiently for Beau and his father to drive off in their big Ford Super Crew before she tossed the shovel aside and gave up on the hope of getting any work done. Eli was due to leave for the day so she had him help her pack up the equipment before sending him on his way.

She sensed multiple stares aimed at her and hoped they were her imagination, not the start of gossip. With any luck, maybe the crews would think she'd discussed Dean's actions with the owners of Buchanan & Son and quit hassling her.

Marley climbed into her truck and sat a moment. She had calls to make and paperwork to do, one last product order to place for her entry in South Ridge's upcoming Winter Festival and—

What was Beau doing here?

Rolling through town, she picked up lunch enroute to the garden center. Not because she was hungry but because she was determined to stick to her routine and be as normal as possible. As though she hadn't just seen the grim specter of her past.

If nothing else, taking a break before her two o'clock appointment would give her a chance to pull herself together. She hoped so. She hated that her hand still shook from the shock of meeting up with Beau again. Hated that he still had that much of an impact on her.

Five bad designs later, Marley tossed her pencil aside and slouched in her office chair, her lunch untouched and the panic inside her growing by the second.

How on earth was she going to stop the train wreck

about to happen? Beau was here. In South Ridge. Near her family.

The phone rang and she jumped at the sound. Amy, the woman she'd hired to work the garden center, was busy outside watering the stock. "Marley's Treehouse."

A pause came from the other end. "You're still upset. Would you like me to call back later?"

She closed her eyes and tried to ignore the surge of awareness that shot through her at the pitch of Beau's voice. Had it always held that gravelly tone? "Never would be better. I'm busy."

"I won't take long," he murmured, sounding drowsy and sexy.

An image popped into her head, one of Beau astride his Harley, a bad-boy grin on his face as he asked her to take a ride. Climbing on the back of that bike had been the biggest mistake of her life.

"I was going to wait to talk to you again until the next time I saw you in person."

"Why didn't you?"

"Because I thought this way might be easier."

"You thought wrong. I refuse to let you upset me—"

"I don't want to upset you, I just want to talk to you. I need answers."

"That's tough. You're not going to get them from me. Leave me alone."

The outer door opened with a jingle of the attached bell.

"I've got to go, I've got a customer."

"They can wait. Just tell me—"

"No. I don't want to talk to you, in person *or* on the phone. We've been over for a long time so leave it that way and don't contact me again."

"Look, I'm sorry I hurt you. I wish I could remember what I did, but if you help me—"

"*Help* you? You've got to be kidding me." She bit her lip and lowered her voice, hoping whoever had walked in hadn't heard. She was so sick of being nice. "When I needed your *help,* you left me high and dry. Go sit and spin, Beau—but *leave me alone.*" Marley hit the off button and slammed the phone down on the desk, inhaling deeply to try to collect herself.

Going out into her display area and being a professional right now would take some doing. Some days—like today—took more effort than others. Some days—definitely today—just *sucked.*

Releasing her breath in a rush, she shook her head at herself. *Get it together. You can't let him get to you or it'll only make things worse.*

Worse? Was that *possible?* Life as she knew it was about to implode and if she didn't—

Footsteps headed toward the office and interrupted her silent rant. Marley raised her head, willing whoever it was away. Two seconds. She just needed two more seconds. "Just a minute! I—I'll be right there!" she called, hoping to buy herself some time. *Deep breath. Deep. Breath.*

"Don't bother," a voice drawled from her doorway. "Especially since it sounds—and looks—like you and I are overdue for some girl talk."

CHAPTER FIVE

"ETHEL?"

"My days of playing Lucy and Ethel are long over." Angel stepped inside, her glamorous red pantsuit and elegant high heels out of place on the rough concrete floor and crates of planter mix. "And if you hadn't had red hair, *I'd* have been Lucy."

Marley grinned. "Ethel was the bomb and absolutely phenomenal in her own right."

"She was the sidekick," her friend complained pointedly, a teasing twinkle in her eyes.

"But sidekicks are very important and—*where* have you *been?*" Marley hopped up from her chair and vaulted bags of perlite to get to Angelique Durand, her best friend since fifth grade when Angel had kept her from being the first to fall asleep at a slumber party thereby risking total humiliation via whipped cream and a frozen bra. "And," she drawled, laughing and hugging Angel close, "if anyone was a sidekick it was me. How *are* you?"

"Just peachy."

Marley held her at arm's length, studying Angel with a critical eye. "Yeah, right, but we'll get into that later. When did you get into town?"

Angel lifted her shoulder in a shrug. "About five minutes ago. I would've been here sooner, but Mr. Johnson was driving his tractor and hay wagon through the four-way. He still has to prove to everybody that he's farming, huh?"

She nodded. "Says he's the only real farmer left in town and not one of the weekenders. I think hauling a load through town on a Wednesday afternoon is his way of proving it." She got down to business. "I've called and called. Why haven't you returned any of my messages?"

"I've been celebrating."

One look told Marley that was a lie, but she didn't press it. She smoothed her friend's straight, white-blond hair back from her face. It hung midway down Angel's back in one of those styles most women would kill to have because it looked so fabulous. If she wasn't such a good friend and person, Marley might have been jealous of Angelique like a lot of other girls in school. But she *was* a good person and Marley had seen firsthand how Angel's appearance had caused her more problems over the years than joy.

"He's crazy, Angel. You didn't deserve what Damon did to you. No one does. How are things, any better?"

"I got the car and a huge settlement, plus court costs and a tidy sum of alimony." She smirked. "Seeing his face when the judge handed that decision down eased the pain considerably, and since he'd publicly declared on numerous occasions he didn't want me working, the judge says he has to keep me in the manner to which I've grown accustomed." She tilted her head to the side, her two-carat diamond studs flashing in the sunshine streaming through the window. "But let's talk about this place. Your decorating skills suck. Where's the bling?" Angel surveyed the office with a grimace.

Marley dropped her hands to her hips. "Hey, you complain and you get put in charge of fixing the problem yourself. Go for it."

"I just might," Angel mused. "But first—who were you talking to when I came in?"

"Uh, no one?"

"Payback for not returning those calls?"

Marley groaned. "It's a long story."

"Yeah, well, I've got nothing but time now."

She glanced at her watch in relief. "You might, but I don't. Rain check for later? I've got a two o'clock I've got to get to, but before I go— You rooming with me?"

"Is that an invitation?"

"Absolutely."

"Then I accept." Angel made a face. "But I would like to lie low for a while. Could you not say anything about seeing me just yet?"

"Done." Marley grabbed a file from her desk. "Now I have to run."

"Haven't you become quite the little businesswoman," Angel drawled, watching Marley search for her keys, calendar and product books. "What do the high-and-mighty people of South Ridge say now that their fallen princess is listed in the Yellow Pages?"

Marley snorted and kept hunting. "Let's just say I think a few of them get off on seeing me on my knees in their front yards."

"Ouch."

"Yeah…" Marley shrugged and tried to pretend her pride wasn't dented. "But so long as they pay me and I can pay my bills, who cares, right? What about you? Any idea what you want to do now that you can join the dregs of the working class again?"

"I haven't decided yet."

"You could always resurrect Delilah Kane."

Surprise crossed Angel's face. "I haven't thought about my on-air alter ego in ages."

"Really? Well, maybe it's time to bring her to life again. Think about it—Delilah's gotten better and smarter with age and come into her own." She found what she needed and gave Angel a smile. "She could really give her listeners an earful now, especially about the problems that come from marrying her boss. And," Marley stressed, "I did just hear that due to a nasty divorce the radio station's owner is looking to sell. Sounds a little desperate, too, since the price has dropped a couple times."

Angel shook her head, but her expression said she was more than a little interested in the news.

Marley's hand tightened over her keys. "Are you sure you're okay?"

Angel tried to smile, but the effort proved too much. Tears glistened her eyes and the moment their gazes met, her casual facade crumpled. "I don't cry over men." Despite her words, the tears overflowed.

"I mean, how stupid— I'm fine, I—I just—" She tilted her head back and inhaled raggedly. "Why didn't I use Delilah's brain and tell him what he could do with his marriage proposal? He played me, Marley, and I let him do it."

"It happens to all of us, but things will get better."

Angel rolled her eyes. "How bad has the gossip been? Be honest."

Unwilling to lie, she grimaced. "You know how the old biddies are. Once they heard, they brought up everything you ever did from birth to the day you left and made up what you did after moving to Chicago, but coming back just means you'll show them what kind of woman you've turned out to be."

Angel nodded firmly. "I will show them. Because I'm fine. Really."

Uh-huh. Angel was about as fine as Marley was with the news that Beau was back in town. "You know what, let me make a phone call. I can cancel my two o'clock."

"No, absolutely not. I'm not doing this now. You don't have time for me to go off about Damon. Certainly not surrounded by all this— What *is* this stuff anyway?"

"Mostly dirt—and a few early Christmas arrivals for the shop."

"Dirt?" Angel laughed, her voice thick. "See what I mean? What a waste. Women with stories like ours need chocolate, a bubble bath and a man—and not in that order."

Marley blinked up at her friend in surprise. "You're still in the market after everything that happened?" She wasn't. After Beau had wrecked her life, the last thing she ever wanted was to find herself taken in by a man's lies again.

"Let's just say I've gotta get back on the horse and bite the hand that bit me and all that."

Once again the door to the outer showroom opened, the bell tinkling loudly. Two seconds later footsteps entered, the tread too heavy to belong to Amy.

"It's the hand that fed you, not bit you."

"Whatever."

She laughed. "Stay here, and don't bite anything. I'll get rid of whoever it is."

"Too late," her brother muttered from the doorway. "Marley, do you—Angelique?"

Keeping her back to him, Angel fluttered her fingers in a sardonic wave and blinked furiously in an effort to get herself under control before Clay saw her tears.

Marley stepped forward and placed herself between them, deciding that she had to set up a barrier in her showroom, something that would slow visitors down and give her a chance to head them off before they made it into her office if Eli or Amy weren't around. "Did you need something?"

Ignoring her completely, Clay stepped around her, not stopping until he stood in front of Angel.

"You mean to tell me that's your car out— What the—" He grasped Angel's arm when she tried to move away. "What's wrong? What happened?"

Angel wiped her eyes with her long, perfectly manicured fingers and smiled. "Nothing. The Roadster has a scratch," she drawled. "You know how us shallow *gold diggers* are. We can't stand it when our toys are damaged." She pulled her arm out of his grip.

"Angelique—"

Angel turned on her spiked heels and walked her model's walk to the door. "Later, Lucy."

"Where's she going?" Clay demanded as the bell sounded again, indicating Angel's exit. "Why was she crying?"

Marley crossed her arms over her chest. "Why do you care?"

He muttered an obscenity that would've sent their mother to bed for days. "What's going on, Mar?"

Fed up with her day, she gave Clay her best all-men-are-idiots glare. "Sorry, can't help you. You want to know something—ask her yourself."

"She won't talk to me."

"Gee, wonder why?" she asked, layering the sarcasm on thick. There were times when her brother ranked right up there with Beau Buchanan. "Did you need something?"

"Yeah, but…"

She raised her eyebrows to prod him on. "But?"

"I came to get flowers."

Didn't that just figure? He'd come to buy flowers for someone else, and yet after seeing Angel, he couldn't focus for wanting to know all about her.

Marley added her brother to her rapidly growing list of Things That Suck. "I don't do rose bouquets in pretty paper, which you should know. Just because I'm a woman in a male-oriented business doesn't mean—"

"I know, I know—I forgot." His gaze narrowed. "What's with you?"

Choking on the angry speech about how all guys were jerks, Marley shoved her hair off her forehead. "Nothing."

"It's obviously something. Come on, what's wrong?"

"Nothing, seriously. I'm sorry. I shouldn't have jumped down your throat. It's just been a bad morning." She managed to hold Clay's gaze, but it was difficult. "Everything is fine. But I've got to go because I'm really, really late."

"Are you sure nothing is wrong?"

She inhaled and sighed. "I stopped by the house today." Marley skipped over the subject of Beau entirely because she just couldn't face that problem yet. Mrs. Conley waited, but if she hurried, she'd still have time to make it.

"And?"

"Mom's getting worse."

Clay's expression softened. "I was afraid that might be it. What happened?"

"What always happens? I bought her a beautiful sunflower because she loves them and…nothing. I barely got a thank-you."

"So she didn't jump up and down clapping her hands because you brought her a present. That doesn't mean she's getting worse. Maybe she's just having an off day."

"It's not that and you know it. Or if it is, every day is an off day lately. You haven't noticed?"

He shook his head. "I haven't been around much,

though, and when I stop by she's usually asleep. I don't want to disturb her so I hang out with Dad."

"Don't you think sleeping all the time is a problem? I can't help but think she's going into that funk where… What if she's on the verge of another collapse?" It hurt to say the words aloud, to admit the fear because it made it more real. Especially now. Could Beau's timing be *worse?*

"I'm sure she's fine. She hasn't been asleep every time I stopped by. Maybe it's you." He held up his hands when her mouth dropped open. "I mean, you as in you're misunderstanding her moods or something, not *you* you."

He had it right the first time. Marley toed the rough floor and glanced at her watch. No way would she make it to her two o'clock now. And she *still* hadn't had lunch. A complaint her gurgling stomach told her quite loudly.

"Just give her some space and stop watching her like a hawk. That's probably what it is," Clay said with a nod. "Maybe she's not comfortable because she knows you watch her so closely. It does get a little much when you get that look on your face—yeah, that one."

She walked over and grabbed the phone. "You're talking to me about looks and *space?* Oh, you mean, like the kind you gave Angel a few minutes ago?"

Her brother's brows pulled low. "I can't talk to her?"

"Not right now, no. You barged in here and immediately started hounding her."

"I didn't hound her. And why can't I talk to her? If not now then when? When she shows up again in another four years?"

Her brother's desire to talk to Angel was the same as Beau wanting to talk to her, but what were her brother's motives? Beau wanted answers because he supposedly couldn't remember. What did Clay want?

Considering Angel's sex kitten body and the relationship they'd once had—which Angel actually blushed over whenever it was brought up—Marley had a pretty good idea. "Guess it's a good thing she's only passing through then, huh?"

Technically it wasn't a lie. Angel didn't know what she wanted at the moment, but Marley sincerely doubted her friend would stay more than a few weeks so *passing through* was accurate.

Clay's eyes widened at the news, and a split second and a curse later, he took off out the door.

Watching him, Marley shook her head. Now she had to make two calls. One to Angel's cell to warn her and another to her two o'clock to say she'd be late.

Men. The world would be a lot quieter and calmer without them.

CHAPTER SIX

BEAU TRIED to get comfortable on his bed. It didn't work. He tossed and turned, wrestling with the pillow and the scratchy sheet that kept him from getting cool in the air-conditioning.

Finally he figured out the mattress was just too soft. Why hadn't he switched it for a firmer one? He'd have to remember to talk to Pop about it later. At least slide a board beneath it to firm it up. Had his tastes changed that much while he was in the Marines?

Beau rolled over onto his back for the tenth time and pulled the pillow over his forehead with a sigh. After a while, his thoughts began drifting, the medicine he'd taken after getting home making him woozy. To distract himself from the pain, he concentrated on imagining Marley and discovered it an easy thing to do.

She'd looked so fierce. Green eyes flashing, her body quivering in surprise at the sight of him even though she'd tried her hardest not to show it. The sun in her hair, a kaleidoscope of reds and golds and blond, but mostly red. A deep, dark red. Red as the devil's tail...

"Red as the devil's tail and probably just as hot, just like Pop says, huh? What do you think? Do you like it?"

"Bet she'd do good, all right."

"Come on, I'll pay you back! You know I will. You've got the money, but it'll be gone if I wait to save it up. Buy it for me. Come on, Joe, please?"

Beau flinched, rolling onto his side and curling his knees toward his chest as bright lights flashed in front of his eyes and sent rockets of pain through his skull.

Cradling his forehead in his good hand, he struggled to raise his injured arm to his head, as well, rubbing, pressing, the sweat breaking out on his body turning icy and making him shiver.

Another memory, another voice.

Hesitant to trigger the gut-clenching pain again, he tried to pull the memory back so he could focus on the details. Tried to put a face with the name and voice, but only saw a filmy haze. The pain lessened bit by bit and after a few more minutes he welcomed the comforting softness of the mattress he'd found so irritating moments before, floating… He pulled the sheet up and eased into the depths with a sigh.

Joe…Joe.

Who the hell was Joe?

THAT EVENING Marley looked through the peephole of her apartment door before unlocking it and swinging it wide. "You're just in time. Dinner will be here in ten minutes."

Angel carried a bag on her shoulder and pulled another suitcase behind.

"Only two?"

"What can I say, the trunk's not that big. Until I decide what to do, I'm traveling light."

Marley laughed. Her friend had a clothes fetish that would rival any Hollywood star.

"I parked between your truck and the building. If Clay comes by tonight, I'm hoping he won't see my car." Angel propped her bags against the wall and released a weary sigh.

"That bad, huh? How was she?"

"Drunk and belligerent, how else? My mother's turned four-letter words into a new language. I learned a few new ones while I was there."

"I'm sorry."

Angel waved a hand in the air. "Don't be. It'll make for a good memoir one of these days."

Marley shut the door and locked it, leaning against the panel while she surveyed her friend. By outward appearance Angelique had it all, but inwardly…

"Come on. Fill me in on the details while I make us some tea."

"QUIT STARING AT ME. I'm fine now. The headache is gone."

Barry nodded and grabbed a biscuit from the KFC box. He knew exactly what was on his son's mind. That woman from the construction site had been on his mind all day, too. It was a given that they'd run into one of Beau's friends or girlfriends before he regained his memory, but who would've thought it would happen in this sleepy river town? "Why do you keep rubbing your neck?"

His son lifted his uninjured shoulder in a shrug. "My mattress is too soft. I slept wrong and have a kink in it now. Think the construction guys would mind me taking some sheeting they're not going to use? I thought I'd put a piece under it to firm it up."

Frowning, Barry reached out to grab the glass of ice water from the table in front of him. "Don't think that would be a problem, but that mattress is practically brand-new. I bet we went to five different stores to find one you liked." He shook his head, picturing the scene.

"What?"

Shaking his head once more, he waved his fork at his son. "You, that's what." He took another drink. "We'd go to look at mattresses and you'd bring a girlfriend. Well, we finally find one, I go to pay, and when I came back, you and she were rolling around making a spectacle of yourself there in the store. Thought we'd have to buy the display model."

Barry blinked when he thought he saw color creeping into his son's face. Embarrassed? Not likely. Beau had stretched out on the bed and grinned cockily, uncaring what the manager had thought or that he'd mortified his father.

"Sounds like you let me get away with too much."

What started off as a chuckle turned into a booming laugh the likes of which he hadn't released in a long, long time. He ended up wheezing and coughing, unable to catch his breath. "Think so, eh? The docs warned me you'd have some personality changes after that conk to your head, but I never dreamed they'd be this drastic. Back then you always told me I was too strict and to leave you alone so you could live your own life. Now I *let* you do it? Parents get the blame for everything, don't they?"

Giving in to the need, he pulled his inhaler from his pocket and took a puff. He had to get back onto a regular schedule. Working so much, being overseas and then trying to catch up, he'd gotten off track with his meds. Now he was starting to feel the effects.

"Probably." Beau searched his gaze for a long moment. "You really don't remember Marley Pierce?"

"I already told you, I don't. Now, eat. That was a doozy of a headache you had today, and I'm thinking it's too soon for you to be doing so much. Maybe you'd better stay around here tomorrow."

Beau picked at his food. "No way. If I have to stare at that ugly wallpaper anymore I'll lose it. I'm coming with you. I promise I'll take it easy."

He raised his eyebrows and waited, expectant even though Beau had generally ignored rules since the beginning of his adolescence.

His son released a long-suffering sigh. "Fine. I'll stay away from Marley Pierce, too."

Barry kept his surprise to himself. Maybe getting hit on the head had changed his son for the better.

THE NEXT DAY Marley used a shovel to dig out a particularly large blackberry root she'd rototilled into submission, and wondered once again at the odds of Beau Buchanan turning up in her hometown.

The previous night had been spent ignoring phone calls from her brother and talking to Angel about

Damon until the early hours of the morning. Angel had a truckload of emotional baggage weighing on her from her marriage, and despite her friend's blasé attitude, Marley knew Angel hurt way more than she let on. That's why she didn't want to add to Angel's worries by mentioning Beau's presence in town.

Laughter and ribbing from the house next door had her discreetly glancing over at the Buchanan crew and noting Beau wasn't among the group of men taking advantage of the shade under the breezeway. The smell of sawdust, the shrill sound of saws and the punch of nail guns filled the air, intermixed with hammers and drills from the third house going up half an acre away.

South Ridge was only about a hundred fifty miles from Cincinnati, and the new development going up on rolling, fertile farmland was certainly large enough to have attracted attention from bidders that far away but…

Here? She'd been by the site numerous times over the last couple weeks while the first house was built and the inside work was being completed, and she'd even noticed the Buchanan & Son trucks parked outside, but she'd never linked the two together.

The Beau she'd known back in Cincinnati had been more apt to party than work, and he'd never mentioned anything about wanting to become an electrician. The mean part of her wondered if he'd have a job if not for his father, but then she reminded herself he was a military vet and an injured one at that and she felt guilty for being so cruel.

The point is you never really knew him.

Marley grimaced at the truth. She'd been away from home for the first time ever, and determined to show her parents she was an adult. A woman ready for college and to be on her own. Instead she'd proven all their doubts and comments about her gullible nature true because she'd believed Beau's smooth-talking lies.

The effects of her sleepless night caught up with her in the form of a loud, unstoppable yawn. She was dog tired and running on nothing but caffeine and worry. Having to face the source of her humiliation certainly didn't make her want to do anything other than go to bed and pull the covers over her head.

Construction was scheduled to last a full two years. *If* it remained on schedule. If not, it would last longer. How many construction jobs remained on schedule?

She stopped to stretch her back for the thousandth time, and hoped for a breeze to ease the anxiety-ridden muscle aches plaguing her. Shaking her head, she made a mental list of possibilities.

Her mom didn't get out much and didn't talk to her friends very often. Clay was seriously distracted by Angel's sudden return, and although she did feel bad about using Angel to her advantage in this case, she was desperate enough to do it. Which left…her father.

"I'm doomed."

Her father worked in South Ridge's most prominent law firm, and belonged to various clubs and organizations. No way would he not hear the construction happenings and gossip when his golf buddies were the development's backers. Was there any way he'd do the same thing she had and not connect the last names? Surely there were plenty of Buchanans in every phone book?

Her frustration grew. She'd worked so hard to make up with her parents. To overcome the embarrassment she'd caused them and be the "good girl" they'd always demanded she be. But none of it would matter now.

The stubborn blackberry vine had more roots than Medusa had snakes. Another one lay before her, half in and half out of the ground. It had taken her five minutes to loosen it as much as it was and the stupid thing still wasn't out. After jabbing it a final time with the shovel, she balanced herself on one hand, shoved her gloved fingers into the ground beneath it, made a fist around it and pulled.

When that didn't work, she rearranged her legs and feet, blew her hair out of her face and used both hands, yanking, *wrenching,* until the root came loose with a spray of sandy dirt that sprinkled her eyes and sent her sprawling backward onto the newly bricked path.

Well, that was graceful.

Marley opened her gritty eyes but quickly squeezed them shut again when pain stabbed through her pupils with the sharpness of a knife. "Oh! *Ow!*"

A rough "Hold on" sounded from close by, and even though the voice belonged to the last person she wanted to see, Beau's presence rid her of the urge to shed a few tears—at least those born of pity. Anger and pain-ridden ones on the other hand…

She rolled to her side and tried to open her eyes again. It didn't work.

"Hang on and don't move."

She felt Beau kneel next to her, his hand on her shoulder urging her onto her back.

"Let go, I've got dirt in my eyes."

"I know, let me— Would you hold still? Lie back."

"I need water to wash them out!"

"Lucky for you I've got some. Settle down and I'll rinse them for you."

"I can— *Hurry.*" Miserable, hot and embarrassed, Marley did as ordered. Calloused fingertips brushed the dirt from the skin around her eyes before settling on her forehead.

"Open your eyes and I will."

She tried, she really did, but between the stinging and the dirt, she couldn't hold them open for more than a second. The hand on her forehead shifted and she felt Beau's thumb settling lower, pulling her lids up. Vaguely, a part of her wondered how he'd manage with the sling but—

"This might hurt a little."

"Wh—"

Cold water splattered onto her face, dousing one eye and then the other before she had time to do more than gasp and sputter. Jerking her head away, she rolled back to her side and sat up, struggling to breathe since water had also gone up her nose. Blinking Marley bit back the litany of names she wanted to call him and grabbed the hem of her shirt, pulling it up to dab at her eyes. "Did you have to *drown* me?"

"You're welcome."

The sound of his voice so close to her ear had her

jerking her head up, and noticing two things at once—the sling was missing from around his neck, and Beau's gaze was focused on her belly. She shoved the now-grimy material down. "Stop that."

Remaining where he was, Beau tilted his dark head to the side and smiled. Oh, that smile.

"You okay now?"

She felt her face heat again. "Fine. Thank you for the, um, water."

Amusement sparkled in his eyes, and he had a grin the likes of which her mama had warned her about.

Too bad she hadn't listened.

"Glad I was around to help."

Marley stood, automatically pulling at her water-spotted shirt because it stuck to her skin.

Beau pushed himself to his feet and he'd almost made it fully upright when he shifted his weight in deference to his injured leg, and slipped. He went down with a muffled sound and landed hard.

Marley's hand flew to her mouth. "Are you all right? *Beau?*"

The pause that followed was broken only by his rough groan. One that didn't sound pain oriented but... Was he embarrassed?

"Um... Let me help you." She grabbed the shovel and held it out to him, thinking he could use it for leverage, but called herself heartless and tossed it aside. She extended her hand instead. "Come on, it's not every day a guy falls at my feet," she quipped, earning a reluctant smile. Heat suffused her cheeks and her conscience niggled that she shouldn't be flirting with him.

Flirting? She *wasn't* flirting.

"Take my hand and let's get you up—er, I mean…" Oh, what had she said! "On your f-feet." Head down and face blazing hot, she ignored the *zing* of sensation that traveled up her arm when he chuckled at her words and placed his larger palm against hers.

Beau used her as a counterbalance as he stood, holding her close for a split second before she came to her senses and backed away. She looked at the roots covering the cracks between the brick and groaned. Two steps forward and four steps back. She'd have to get those cleaned out or else be called back in the spring to fix it when the roots began to grow.

"Marley—"

"I've got to get back to work. Thanks for the save with my eyes." When he opened his mouth to argue she cut him off again. "There's no use pretending we're anything other than what we are, Beau—and that's not friends. You made that clear a long time ago."

"I don't remember that."

"Too bad. I do."

He stared at her a long moment, his expression thoughtful. Remorseful? Guilt stirred at her uncaring words. What would it be like to not remember? His expression bothered her. So much so that for a rash second, she wanted to forget the past and…play nice.

Marley turned her back to him and grabbed the shovel. No way should she be thinking *nice* when it came to Beau Buchanan. *Nice* wasn't smart. In fact, being nice would be royally *stupid.*

She didn't hear Beau walk away, but she knew the moment he was no longer there. The awareness was gone. The tension.

Shaking her head, she got back to work.

She'd been nice once.

And she knew better than anyone that nice girls finished last.

CHAPTER SEVEN

AN HOUR OR SO LATER Clay pulled into the driveway. Marley had finished preparing the ground on the far side of the house for shrubs and had started planting them when her brother got out of his Jeep, wearing a fierce scowl. She stopped, taken aback because he looked so much like their father. Great, just what she needed. Had he heard?

Grabbing a boxwood, she positioned it and did her best to act casual.

"What's this I hear about you getting it on with some guy in broad daylight?"

Mouth agape, she twisted to face him, scraping her knee on a rock in the process. "*What?* Who said that?" Marley turned toward the nearby construction trailer, and sure enough, the general contractor's secretary had her face pressed to the glass watching them. "Kallie *called* you?"

"Actually, I called her to let her know I'd be stopping by to take pictures before the storms hit later in the week. I asked how you were doing and she said—"

"That I was getting it on with a guy. Of all the—" She made a face. "I got *dirt* in my eyes and couldn't see anything. One of the—the guys rinsed them for me."

"That all?"

"Yes!" She glanced over at the trailer's window to find Kallie conspicuously absent.

"If that's all, then why are you getting so bent out of shape?"

"Because." She forced herself to take a deep breath. "Because she told you that. That's how nasty rumors get started and I don't appreciate her saying it, even if she was joking." *Which she wasn't.*

"Sounded to me like she was happy for you."

"Yeah, right. If anything she was trying to milk you for information about who he was."

"She thought you had a boyfriend."

"I don't."

"Okay, fine, no boyfriend. I still think I'll go over there and say thanks. You know, be brotherly."

She so didn't like the twinkle in his eye when he said that.

Marley laughed, but it sounded forced to her own ears. When Clay's eyebrow hiked up behind his sunglasses and he shot her a know-it-all smirk, she said a quick prayer. "Get real. Wh-why would you want to do that? It was no big deal."

He hesitated, his gaze narrowing. "You're lying. Why are you lying?"

"I'm not."

"Think I can't tell?" His expression turned superior. "You're a horrible liar, but you're giving it your best shot which means…something's going on here." He crossed his arms over his chest. "You going to tell me what it is, or do I have to go over there and find out for myself?"

Kallie's face reappeared in the window.

Marley ignored the woman as best she could and released another weak laugh. "You've always had an overactive imagination. You should be writing novels instead of newspaper articles." She grabbed a shrub and turned away from him. "Hey, while you're here, look at these and tell me if they're spaced correctly. I set my yardstick down and someone swiped it."

In response to her words, Clay turned on his loafered heel, his direction clear.

"Clay." Marley couldn't believe her luck when she heard the familiar rumble of a diesel engine pulling onto development property. Not long after helping Beau to his feet, she'd noticed him leaving with his father. Not that she'd been watching for him, she'd simply wondered if he'd been hurt. Regardless, the truck was back, which meant Beau might be getting out any second and— "Clay, *wait!*" She tossed the plant aside.

Too late. She knew the moment her brother spotted the Buchanan & Son sign on the truck. The *instant* Clay recognized the name and things clicked. Desperate, Marley jogged the last few feet separating them and tossed herself at his back, wrapping her arms around his shoulders dirt and all, letting her weight drag at him from behind.

"What the— *Let go.*"

"You are *not* going over there. This isn't the playground and I handled it myself."

"It's—"

"I know good and well who it is," she hissed into his ear, "and you are *not* going over there!" Marley raised a hand and smacked him gently on the back of his head, hoping it would knock some sense into him.

"Stop that," he growled, glaring at her over his shoulder. "The truck—"

"It's a company truck." She prayed hard that Barry Buchanan had dropped Beau off somewhere, that Beau wasn't about to climb out of the passenger side because if he did… "Stop pulling the older-brother act, will you?"

Clay stared across the street. Barry parked and got out, carrying takeout for his men. And while seemingly a nice enough man, Barry was quite a bit older and not her type, which Clay knew very well. Thankfully, no one else emerged.

Her brother inhaled deeply. The anger keeping his shoulders tensed subsided in slow degrees. She swallowed and let go. Dirt had stained his dress shirt, but given his less-than-stellar mood, she wasn't about to mention it and get him started on a lecture about her behavior. A lecture that would inevitably lead back to Angel's influence over her. Her brother loved the hoyden in Angel. With his little sister, he just considered it problematic.

Maybe no one would notice?

"You're digging yourself in deep, Marley."

"I haven't done anything."

"He's—"

"A guy who came to town to work on the housing development. Nothing else."

"You're going to want my help when this blows up in your face."

No doubt she was. Did that mean he offered it?

"But you're not going to get it."

"Clay—"

"Not when I know Angel's still in town and you're hiding her. Where is she? Angelique might go to see her mom, but she wouldn't stay there and she didn't check into any of the hotels in the area. That leaves you. She's at your apartment, isn't she?"

"I have no idea what you mean."

"Really? How was dinner last night? I ran into Mr. Chang this morning and he asked me if I'd enjoyed the takeout, said you'd bought dinner for two. You invite that guy?" He jerked a thumb toward the house across the street.

"Of course not! I was just hungry because I missed lunch. If you must know, I ordered too much and there's leftovers in my fridge." That part wasn't a lie.

Clay bent until he was nearly nose to nose with her. "You bought Crab Rangoon even though you hate it?" Hands propped on his hips, he frowned down at her and waited.

Mr. Chang must've gone into detail. Or else Clay had suspected and asked. "She's there." Marley figured it wouldn't hurt to confirm the obvious. Clay knew Angel wouldn't stay anywhere else but with her.

Her brother nodded once. "I'll deal with you and Angel later, but for now… Where is he?"

She lifted her chin. "I don't know where he went and I don't care. Neither should you."

"How do you figure that?"

"Clay, please don't make this *worse*. You're right, okay? I'm going to need help, but if Dad has to come bail you out of jail again because you've gotten in a fight over me, Mama won't talk to me for *another* two years! Let me handle this and—and *back me up*."

Marley walked over to where she'd been planting, the walkway littered with dirt and the remains of the stubborn blackberry vine she'd unearthed. She'd have to remember to remind Eli to remove them from the topsoil mix before shaping the beds.

"Get the bad stuff out, Marley, don't let it hide only to come out and ruin everything."

She'd learned that on her knees beside her mother, digging in the backyard, and while she loved her mom, knew somewhere deep inside her mother loved her in return, there was a monstrous gap to mend and Beau Buchanan's presence would make that impossible. *What was she going to do?*

"He was the guy who rinsed your eyes, wasn't he? You *talked* to him?"

"Just for a second." Clay didn't need to know there had been more than one collision between her and Beau. "It was more me gaping at him in shock, and then telling him to stay away from me, but I took care of things."

"How do you figure that when he's still here?"

"It's complicated." That sounded lame even to her.

"You'd better uncomplicate it and come up with a good defense because when Mom and Dad find out, you're—"

"It's not like I asked him to come here. And it's a free country. I can't make him leave, not without stirring up more talk by trying to attempt it." She smoothed her damp hair back off her face and rubbed her still-itchy, watery eyes. "Beau and his father are the owners of the electrical company doing the wiring for the development. No, I didn't know that when I bid on the job," she stressed, answering the question she figured he'd ask next. "But they are, they're under contract and they're going to be here until the project is done. Do you think Beau's going to screw up a legally binding *contract* because once upon a time he—"

"Screwed you?"

Frustrated tears blurred her eyes once more, but she determinedly blinked them away. "I was going to be a little more tactful, but yeah." Lifting her hands, she wiped the sweat from her forehead and groaned. "Put yourself in my shoes for a minute. I didn't plan this. I don't *want* this, but what am I going to do? Mama will go over the edge if she finds out."

"She's not going to like this, but she's not getting worse. It just takes her time to cope with things."

"It's been *years*. This is going to stir it all up again and people will talk." Clay was quiet a long moment and Marley could practically see his mind working through the mess.

"Okay. Something in your favor is that she hardly

goes anywhere anymore. Maybe she won't hear about it."

"With the likes of Kallie and Mr. Chang around? I don't think so." She swooped down and grabbed a knot of crabgrass by its roots, tossing it into the wheelbarrow a few feet away. "Most people won't remember or connect the name, but Mama and Dad's friends certainly might."

"I don't think Mom's friends are just going to call her up and tell her about that guy after what happened. They'd hesitate because of her breakdown and not want to be the blame for a relapse."

Like her. "Maybe." Rubbing a spot of mud caked to her hand, she glanced at him. "Did you know she's seeing Dr. Bourke now?"

He frowned. "I thought she saw Dr. Myners?"

"She told me Bourke yesterday. And there was Dr. Ramsey for a little while before that. I could've sworn she went to see him not that long ago. Clay, I'm telling you, she's acting different, even compared to before. More…distant. Out of it. I can tell, and I can't believe you can't."

"Will you get off it, she's fine."

Marley released a heavy sigh and wished she could believe him. "Nothing is fine. Everything's about to blow up."

Her brother nodded, his expression grim. "Probably so. With him in town, I'd say it's only a matter of time."

"I'll talk to Beau again. See if I can—"

"No," Clay muttered. "You don't talk to him anymore. At all. Got it?"

"If I don't talk to Beau, how do I convince him to leave?"

He ran his hand through his hair. "I don't know," he said with a groan. "All right, do it. But if you do talk to him, make sure it's not in sight of Kallie, otherwise the whole town will know."

Not what she wanted to hear.

"Mar, I'll stand by you, okay? And if he gives you any trouble I want to know about it. I mean it. In exchange, you can help me with Angel."

She smiled sadly. "Clay, I'd love to see the two of you together. I really would. But she needs time."

"She's had time. I screwed up, all right? I know that. I regret that I said all those things to her. But she was dating that jerk and shoving every gift he gave her in my face."

"She grew up with nothing. *Nothing.* Can't you understand why material things appealed? It doesn't make her a bad person."

"I understand that, and I know that's not all there is to her, but it's taken time to calm down and process things after she treated me like that."

"Like what? Are you seriously going to stand there and blame her for dating Damon when you didn't want to be seen in public with her because of where she came from? Have you forgotten *that?*"

Color tinged his cheeks. "I was an ass and a jerk—"

"Go on."

His gaze darkened in anger. "Look, I let so-called friends keep me from seeing how great she was. It was the wrong crowd and now I know better. She's back, she's single and I'd like to make it up to her. See if we can figure things out and start over. Mar… I won't treat her like he did, okay? I…"

"You what?" she asked when he didn't finish whatever it was he'd been about to say. "Clay, her mom is still her mom, the way she grew up—none of that's changed. Before you convince yourself you can handle things, you'd better know for sure that you actually can."

He looked away from her. "I can. I *know* I acted like a jerk before, but everybody should get a second chance. You want one, right? I'd think you'd understand where I'm coming from and be more sympathetic."

She stared at him a long moment, able to see the sincerity in his expression. Finally, she caved. "I can't make any promises."

"Just talk to her. Do what you can to get her to hear my side of things."

"Okay, I will—if you remember that you've promised to help me when the poop hits the fan."

"Deal." Clay gave her a relieved grin. "Now I've got to get back to work. I came by to snap some shots of the houses to do a progression article on the big build. Mind if I take one of you working on the finishing touches?"

"I don't know."

"Come on." He pulled a small digital camera from his pocket and ordered her into a several poses, snapping shots. "Got it."

When he turned to leave, Marley stopped him. "Thanks, Clay. It helps knowing that between you and Angelique I'm not going to go through this alone."

Her brother grinned. Not a sweet, caring grin, but one she remembered from childhood. Full of mischievousness and... "What?"

"Nothing. You're not alone by a long shot, Mar." He laughed softly. "Besides, I wouldn't have missed coming by today for anything."

She narrowed her gaze, confused. "Why?"

"Turn around."

Marley did, gasping when she spied her reflection in the window. Thanks to the dirt and the water used to rinse her eyes she looked like a raccoon—and he'd taken pictures!

"Clayton Douglas Pierce, you give me that camera right—"

"You keep lookin' like that," he called, well on the way to his Jeep, "and I won't have to worry nearly as much about you working out here with him."

"Clay!"

"Call me tonight with an update on Angel—otherwise these get printed."

BEAU RODE WITH POP every morning to the job site but because of storms, he didn't see Marley again until two days later. She rolled in at ten till ten, and he watched from his position inside the house across the street as Marley got out of the landscaping truck and lowered the back gate of the vehicle. Containers of plants, trees and shrubs were inside and between her and the teenage boy, Eli, they had everything unloaded in a matter of minutes.

Marley wore knee-baring cargo shorts and another

Marley's Treehouse T-shirt. The sight of her toned, tanned legs and body outlined by the clothes was enough to have him straining for a closer look. She was beautiful. Sexy in a wholesome, earthy way. So what had happened between them? What had he said? Done? Why wouldn't she talk to him?

Not knowing was driving him nuts.

He'd prepared himself for another boring day without her presence, paced around the house repeatedly, and then finally bucked up his courage and stumbled inside. A panic attack struck the moment he entered the dim interior. He'd had to stay by the door of the building to keep from getting sick, but at least he'd managed to spend the last two hours propped against the frame.

The cold sweats had faded, and he told himself it was progress. But how much? Something about the sight of the two-by-four studs, the supplies, the boxes and buckets and the guys inside…

"Something wrong, son?"

He turned from the door before Pop could take note of what he studied, and cautiously made his way to where his old man wired a breaker box. Twice he had to pause and swallow the surge of unease crawling over him before moving deeper into the interior, one small, forced step at a time. "Think I'll take a walk and get my PT done for the day, stretch my shoulder along the way."

"You keep it up and you'll be healed in no time. Take the cell in case you have a problem and need a lift. Baker's got his on him, so hit star nine to get him." His father paused and shot him a level stare. "You've been here quite a while today, inside to boot. Sure you're not ready to let me drive you home?"

Pop's shrewd gaze slid over him, and he knew his father had seen the tremors and sweats. "I'm sure. I hope to be here longer tomorrow, and for a lot more than playing gofer every time you need a tool from the truck." The words came out sharper than he'd intended and Beau frowned. "Sorry," he murmured, squeezing the tight muscles in his neck. "I'm just ready to get back into things and tired of being in the dark."

Pop nodded his forgiveness. "Soon, son. It'll happen soon."

"I remember electrical work. I don't know how, but it's all there. Just not people."

Pop tossed the pliers aside. "I understand that, but I don't want to see you having a setback if you strain your shoulder or your leg getting up and down wiring this place. Give yourself a few more days. We'll be doing the security system soon. If you're up to it, I'd be glad to have you help."

That was at least a week away and they both knew it. Seven days of roaming around the minuscule house, staring at the walls and watching them close in on him. Maybe he could sneak in another few loads of laundry, something that would help Pop out without being too obvious.

"Go for your walk. The sunshine'll do you good."

Without comment, Beau left the house by the back door and slowly made his way around to the front, hoping that by skirting the side farthest away from his old man, he'd be able to cross the street unnoticed. Maybe if he talked to Marley again the memory of him and her would return, a time frame. Details. *Something.*

Eli was in the process of helping Marley dig a hole for a plant she held at the ready. The kid grinned when he saw him. "Hey, man. Looking better today."

Marley's head snapped up in a flash, her gaze wary.

"Thanks, I feel better. Marley, I was wondering if you could take a break? I could grab some water and—"

"We're busy." She slid Eli a quelling glance when the kid grinned.

"Just five minutes?"

She shook her head. "Can't. We have to get these planted before it rains." Marley set the plant in her hand near the hole and busied herself positioning the rest of the flowers, arranging them here and there by scooting them inches or in the case of one, a few feet.

"Marley—"

"Whoa, sounding desperate, dude," Eli warned.

Beau ground his teeth together. He did sound desperate. Maybe because he was. He was tired of waiting for memories that came too few and too far apart. Memories that didn't make sense because he didn't recognize the voices and couldn't visualize the faces.

He hesitated, hoped she'd change her mind, but when she kept her head down and used a hand shovel to start digging, he took it as his cue.

Before long he'd come to the end of the graveled construction road and the sign marking the entrance to South Ridge Estates. He should probably turn around and go back so that Pop could take him home, but he didn't want to. Didn't want to have to walk by the house where Marley worked, didn't want to feel the interest and attraction he felt for her and know she hated his guts for something, but he didn't know what.

He shook his head, thinking of how good she'd felt the brief time he'd held her hand. The walk helped rid him of the frustration and his leg gradually loosened so he kept going, farther and farther until he'd made it close to home before the muscles began to spasm. Spying a large rock not far off the road, he crossed over the guardrail and headed that way, his thoughts consumed by his lack of memory.

He wanted to be better now. He wanted to remember *now.* To do something to get that worried look off his father's face, to know what he'd done to Marley so he could make up for it.

The Lord's unfailing love surrounds the man who trusts in Him.

The sweat he'd worked up during his walk turned cold. The woman's voice in his head— Oh, God, her voice. He *knew* that voice.

The words rang over and over again in his head, so familiar and yet just out of reach. He heard the love in her tone, the way she'd murmur those words anytime he got upset, anytime he—

His mother. The voice was his *mother's.*

The awareness came in an instant, a flash of knowledge from the vast sea of nothing in his mind. Beau lifted a shaking hand and rubbed his stinging eyes.

His head pounded as though the leak of information was poison to his brain. But for the first time since waking up in the hospital, he welcomed the pain. He might not remember anything else, but he remembered his mother's voice.

Remembered…remembered dark brown hair, almost black, and blue eyes. The way she'd spend every night in her favorite chair, humming and rocking, back and forth. The memory was everything, small in the realm of all he'd lost, but everything just the same.

His foot slid on a rock, but he ignored the corresponding pain in his thigh as the muscles contracted harder. Two steps later he did it again, and groaned at the stab of pain streaking up his thigh and down into his knee. Almost to the rock, his leg buckled under him.

CHAPTER EIGHT

MARLEY JERKED the wheel to get off the road when she saw Beau fall.

He was fine. Fine. So why wasn't he moving?

That moment, that split second, tipped the scales of her grudge and turned it into belly-churning fear. She might not like the man—and she *really* didn't like him—but she didn't want anything to happen to him.

There were poisonous snakes in the area. Copperheads and rattlesnakes who were notorious for sunning themselves on days like this. What was he doing going over there?

She scrambled out of the truck and ran toward him. Beau had shifted and now sat on the ground with his back pressed against the rock, but she could hear his hoarse breathing overtop of her own once she got close enough. Not taking any chances, she scanned the ground as she ran.

"Are you all right?" she asked as she drew near. "Is it your leg? Was it a snake?"

When he heard her speak, Beau's face tightened. "Thought you didn't want to talk to me."

"A woman's prerogative. I'm allowed to change

my mind so shut up." She wished the order had come out strong instead of breathless. "What happened?"

"My leg. No snake."

Thank God. Marley reached out to touch him, to smooth her fingers over his tense features and offer comfort, only to jerk them back short of the mark. Curling them into her palm, she grabbed her cell phone from the waistband of her pants and moaned at her lack of service. She'd meant to pick up one of those booster antennae to help with reception in the dead areas, but she'd put it off as an expense she didn't need. Which meant it was now up to her to get Beau help. "Come on, let's get you in the truck. Put your arm around my shoulders."

A strong breeze blew through the valley and a cloud covered the sun. The loss of the sun's rays sent a shiver over her despite the temperature of the air. Thunder rolled in the distance. Seconds went by and the sun re-emerged.

"I'm fine."

"You're hugging a rock in *pain.*" Thunder rolled again. "Come on, before we get soaked."

"It's easing up. I just overdid it and the muscles cramped up. Go on, I'll be fine."

Yeah, right. If he rubbed his thigh any harder he was going to start a fire from the friction. A grimace marred the lean angles of his face.

Marley fought her impatience and the temptation to do as he asked. "You need to see a doctor and—I can't leave you here like this."

"Why not? You don't want to talk to me."

"I'm talking now, aren't I? Think of this as your big break to grill me. Are you coming with me or not?"

His pain-dazed eyes focused on her face with a searing intensity. She looked away. But breaking eye contact had other consequences. Marley glanced down and realized she hovered over him, both her hands resting on his chest and stomach, well able to feel the hard muscles beneath. She jerked her hands away and clasped them tightly in her lap.

"I'm coming, but no doctor. I'm fine." The words were muttered, and not at all believable uttered as they were between his clenched teeth. "I'll ice it when I get home. It'll be as good as new tomorrow."

She highly doubted it, but she wasn't going to argue for the sake of arguing. By the time she got him on his feet, Marley wondered if Beau had any teeth left. The arduous walk to the truck was an act of sheer will and stubborn determination. Along the way she had to fight hard to ignore the solid feel of his body beside hers, moving against her with every slow, wobbling step.

Memories resurfaced and brought a flush to her cheeks that had nothing to do with the heat, and everything to do with not being the virginal girl she'd been back then. Beau had been a great-looking guy and they'd been good together. But now...Beau's years in the military had hardened him, honed him until he was all muscle and man, and despite her anger and all the pain he'd caused her she couldn't help but notice.

Finally they reached the truck. Marley opened the door then had to balance Beau while he favored the injured leg and the arm so recently in a sling. Fighting off another surge of memories, she plastered herself to his side and helped him by pushing where she could. Doing so put her up-close-and-personal with Beau. He froze in the act of trying to get situated on the bench seat, his gaze fastening on her face, her eyes, before it dropped to her mouth.

Other than the rasp of their breathing and the wind in the trees from the brewing storm, nothing broke the silence surrounding them. Marley couldn't help but think that the growing turbulence in the sky above them reflected the mood, the moment, perfectly. No cars, no noise. There was just the two of them and a lot of things unsaid.

Beau lifted his hand, slowly, to her cheek, his knuckles rough as they grazed lightly over her skin and down, toward her lips. "Marley."

Her name brought her out of her daze. She jerked backward, her panicked momentum stopped when her shoulder blades slammed into the door of the truck.

Beau's expression softened. "Are you okay?"

"Don't touch me."

"Marley… Baby, I'm not—" His eyes widened, the fading bruise at the corner raising slightly with his eyebrows. "You're afraid of me?" He blanched. "Is that it? When we were together, I *hurt* you?"

He looked so horrified and disgusted at the thought, the need to reassure him was automatic. "N-No!" She took a steadying breath. "No, Beau, you didn't hurt me. Not physically."

Beau sagged against the seat in relief. "Thank God."

A muffled laugh erupted from her chest. "God had nothing to do with what we did. Now, where do you want me?" The very second the question left her mouth, she cringed. He unnerved her so badly, and looking the way he did—all concerned and scared and freaked out at the thought of her frightened of him… "To take you," she clarified, belatedly realizing her words only made the double entendre worse. *Where do you want me to* take *you?* Oh, good grief! "To the doctor o-or home?"

"Home." Beau held her gaze and refused to let her look away. "Take me home. We can talk there."

Marley shut the door with a slam, unable to believe he hadn't laughed at her blunders. She took the long way around the truck, the rain-cooled wind whipping her hair out of her band and blowing it in her face, cooling her embarrassment-heated body.

Her attack of foot-in-mouth could only be blamed on the differences in Beau. The way he made her feel hyperaware and on edge. Five years ago Beau was a gorgeous hottie, but now…

Now there was something about him. Something basic and elemental, masculine. Maturity was certainly part of it, but there was still *more.*

She shook her head to clear it. The first drop of cold rain splattered her forehead and broke her out of her musings. Whatever it was, it didn't matter. She'd been there, done that, and she wasn't about to let some sinfully long eyelashes and a rugged set of features send her into blind orbit again. She'd forgotten herself once and then she and her family had paid the price. Beau hadn't just broken her heart, that had been the least of the damage done.

Unable to slow her steps anymore, she made it to the cab of the truck and grabbed the handle to climb inside just as the clouds opened up. Rain poured from the sky. Beau struggled with the task of rolling his window up because of his injury, but she managed with little fuss, leaving a two-inch gap at the top.

Seconds passed and they were trapped inside the too-small cab, both of them sticky with sweat and dirt and rain. Marley started the truck and ground the gears, bit her tongue to still the curse that sprang to her lips and finally got the truck moving.

Beau shifted uncomfortably on the seat. A quick glance at the set of his jaw and the stiff way he moved revealed he was still in pain.

"Thanks for the ride."

Marley ignored him and prayed he'd do the same to her. Rain drummed against the roof of the cab, locked them in the overheated space. She'd told Clay she'd talk to Beau about leaving but now that the time had presented itself, the words refused to come.

"That makes the second time I fell on my butt in front of you." Beau chuckled, the sound edged with wry embarrassment. "Probably a God-smack for whatever it was I did to you."

Her hands tightened on the wheel. *God-smack?* She'd heard the term used many times, believed in them herself after her various experiences, but the so-called gentle reprimands God gave a person when He felt they were getting a tad out of hand and needed to be reminded of who was in control wasn't exactly something she would've associated with Beau. Apparently war had made him religious. "You, um, never struck me as a faith-oriented kind of guy."

Beau sat with his head leaning against the seat, a smile curling his lips up at the corners. "I was that bad, huh?"

Best to stick with the truth. "You were a parent's nightmare and a girl's good time."

"But?"

This time she was the one who laughed. "But what? Those kinds of good times never last."

"Sounds like I didn't deserve to have them last." He hesitated. "Pop said I was ordered to either enlist or serve time. I realize that to have been given the choice between those two options, I wasn't a stand-up kind of guy."

Marley nibbled her inner lip, surprised that he'd admit what he just did and have the grace to look ashamed about it.

Amazing. Five years ago Beau would've bragged about his "badness." Now he said thanks, laughed at himself for supposedly embarrassing himself in front of her and… How could someone change so much?

The old Beau would've copped a feel while she helped him to the truck and taken advantage of her incapacitated state and kissed her before rinsing her eyes. In the two weeks she'd known him five years ago, Beau had always put himself first. His wants, his needs, his desires. Him, him, him. Which made courtesy and common decency from him—*weird.*

"Marley, I need answers."

Ah, there it was. The Beau Factor. She should've known it was coming. He wanted answers, and he was determined to get them. The confession had been to butter her up.

"Do you know where you're going?"

She pulled her gaze from the road long enough to slide him a glare. "No," she admitted softly, "but I've seen your dad coming from this direction so I assume your home is up ahead."

"Next left. Hang a right, then another left." He smiled again. "Was that so bad?"

She didn't respond. They both knew that wasn't what he wanted to talk about.

Marley drove in silence, aware of the way he watched her, waiting for Beau to question her. How did they meet, where. Why did they end. Would he ask that? What would she say? That she'd thought herself in love with him and he didn't love her back? That was just too humiliating to reveal. Much worse than merely admitting she'd had sex with him.

Sweat coated her body and she probably smelled a little ripe, a combination of the heat and humidity and nervousness of being confined with him. She wished she could turn on the air-conditioning, but the truck was twenty years old and the rain-splattered breeze from the lowered windows and side air vents would have to do.

"Marley—"

"I can't." She shook her head quickly back and forth. "I thought I could, but I can't."

"Can't what?"

"I can't do this. Let you grill me. I lied to get you in the truck. Sue me."

"Marley—"

"No, Beau. Can we not *do* this?" Her resolve to be civil slipped, and her hands ached where they gripped the wheel. "Can we just…Beau, drop the act and be honest." She forced herself to meet his gaze. "What will it take for you to leave South Ridge and never come back?"

"Marley, I'm not lying about the memory loss."

"I know that." She wet her dry lips. "It makes it worse, almost, but it certainly doesn't excuse it."

"Excuse *what?* Marley, please, talk to me. Whatever it is I did, I want to make up for it."

"You can't, so why bother talking about it?" She hated the way her name sounded coming from his mouth.

"But you believe me? About the amnesia?"

She nodded. "After you left, the site manager came over to see how things were going. He saw you talking to me and mentioned your dad going to Germany to be with you. He speaks highly of your father, says he's a good guy. If that's true—"

"It is."

"Then he wouldn't make up something like amnesia to excuse your behavior. He wouldn't lie about something that serious—not even for you." Beau *had* lied to her before. Many times. An amazing amount considering the short time she'd known him. But the changes in personality and behavior, well, that fit the descriptions of amnesia she'd read on the Internet last night when she'd been too worried to sleep.

"Pop is a good guy. He stayed by my side at the hospital the whole time I was there."

"That's nice. Parents should do that." Her throat tightened and she cleared it. "They should support their kids and—and be there for them." *The way her mother would never be there for her.*

As if sensing her mood, Beau lifted his uninjured arm to rest along the top of the bench seat. His fingertips brushed her shoulder. "Touchy subject?"

"You could say that."

"Okay… How about some good news then? You'd be the first to know."

She wondered if Beau's change of topic was to be nice or get her to lower her guard. "What good news?"

"I remembered something while I was walking."

Her heart missed a beat. "About us?"

The question slipped out before she could stop it. What a stupid thing to ask. Of course he wouldn't remember anything about them. *They* had barely existed, and only then because she'd allowed Beau to get into her pants when she'd kept other guys at arm's length. A virgin he'd had to have until he'd done the deed and then…

"No. Sorry."

Another apology, she mused. Where had they been back then? "What did you remember?" she asked quickly, wanting to move on.

"It was something my mother used to say. A Psalm she liked to quote. All I could remember at first was the sound of her voice while she said it, but then it sort of repeated in my head a few times and I knew it was her. I even remembered what she looked like."

She smiled at the triumphant expression on his face. "That's great. Congratulations." She would've thought his first memory would've been of a kegger or something similar. How sweet was it that it was of his mother?

Mama's boy. She bit her lip. Apparently even guys like Beau held a soft spot for their mothers.

But a Psalm?

Stop it!

Remembering something was a step in the right direction. One that obviously meant a lot to him. She wouldn't lower herself to being mean about that. What if their situations were reversed? She didn't want to be on the receiving end of a God-smack and find out what that would be like.

"Yeah. I'm pretty happy right now. Maybe it's the start, you know? I've remembered a few other things, voices, but I couldn't identify the people. I just heard them. I'm hoping that since I can remember her voice and what she looked like, the others will come. Who knows, maybe it means I'll remember us soon, too."

Marley pulled her gaze away from his and focused on driving, the silence between them dragging on. "So what do you remember? Other than what you remembered today."

"Nothing specific."

She swung her head back toward him in surprise. "Nothing? As in *nothing?*"

He nodded. "Basic stuff. How to eat, tie my shoes, fix breakfast. Normal stuff people do every day. I can do all of that without a problem, but I don't remember people or the past. It's all gone, like a big blur in my head that I can't get sorted out."

Marley stared out at the road ahead, trying to comprehend the magnitude of such a thing. Thinking of amnesia in technical medical terms was one thing, but to remember nothing? How frightening. Still… "Does it ever seem nice?"

"What do you mean?"

She shrugged. "I can't imagine it all disappearing. Being able to start over again."

"It only disappears if no one else remembers, Marley."

Good point. She mulled over Beau's words while she made the turns he'd told her to take, the silence lengthening as they drove along a narrow back road parallel to a shallow creek. "Do the doctors know when your memory will return?"

He shook his head with a caustic laugh. "They say it'll come back in time, but there's no specific date. I'm supposed to be patient while I get bits and pieces the way I just did, and try to pretend people don't look at me as if I'll go postal at any moment or need to be placed in a home for mental patients."

Stiffening at the comment and the reminders that it brought to the surface, she pulled up to the little house, recently empty due to an elderly woman's passing. Mrs. Addington. The woman had always been outside tending her flowers, a member of the same local gardening club her mother had helped found but no longer belonged to.

Marley was a member now because of her business, but she rarely attended meetings and sat in the back when she did, her mother's friends up front. The sight of them was a constant guilt-trip because her mother wasn't there. Thanks to her.

Marley rubbed her forehead to ease the tension. "Your father can't help you with your questions about the past? Give you hints?"

"About some things, yeah, but the shrinks told him I need to remember on my own so the only things he'll tell me really don't matter much." He leaned closer. "You obviously knew me pretty well."

"What makes you say that?"

His eyes narrowed, the tiny lines at the corners deepening in the process. "I'm not the type of person who needs protecting, Marley. You have things to say to me, I can tell. Say them. I'm stronger than Pop thinks and I need answers, which is why I'm asking you to be honest with me. Marley, tell me what happened with us. How would you handle this if you were me? The not knowing? Could you be this way and be satisfied with everyone telling you to wait?"

She'd hate it. In that regard, she and Beau were similar because she'd react with the same inquisitiveness.

"I know you don't like me now because of whatever happened between us, but I want to fix it. Marley, I'd like a clean slate with you."

Feeling herself softening toward him, she stared out the window at the hydrangea bush whose blooms had started to dry on the stem. She felt like that, still alive but dead, too. Not a part of things because she couldn't integrate herself back into her parents' lives. Not a part of the dating scene because fear always held her back.

No way could she admit to Beau how much of a fool she'd been to believe his lies, to think of them as a couple when she'd been nothing more to him than an easy lay.

She understood his need to know the truth, empathized, but she couldn't go down that path. Not with him. "Do you need help to the door?"

Hesitating only briefly, Beau locked his jaw at her refusal and eased out of the truck into the steady rain.

"Was whatever I did to you that bad?"

She smiled, tired. "You need to go in. Don't forget to ice your leg."

He didn't move. "I meant what I said, Marley. I'm sorry. I can tell I hurt you, but if we could talk about it and put whatever happened behind us, we could start over. It could be nice."

Her heart lurched at his words, at his coaxing smile. Marley shoved the vehicle into Reverse and shook her head. "I don't think so. B-besides, you said you need to remember on your own."

"Marley, talk to me. Come inside. We'll—"

"No. I can't do this, Beau. Do you think I don't want to go back and have a do-over? You screwed up my life, and no matter how hard I try to make up for it, I'm *still* paying the price."

"What does that mean? *What did I do?*"

"Just let it be!"

"I can't! Do you think I haven't figured out that if it wasn't important, you'd have already told me? That if it was some stupid kid stuff, it would be no big deal and you'd spit it out? But it was a big deal, I see it on your face. In your eyes. I'm not going to stop asking, Marley, not until you tell—"

"I was pregnant." Even though she'd barely had a voice to say the words, he heard them. A derisive laugh escaped her chest at his shock. "You look so surprised." Her throat burned, so tight it felt as if a knot had formed on her vocal cords. She'd told Beau this before and he hadn't cared. How cruel was it that she had to go through it again?

"We have a baby?"

A sound escaped her, full of every ounce of pain she had inside her. "No, Beau, we don't. We don't have anything and we never did. You made me *pregnant,* but you didn't give a damn about either one of us. Shut the door."

"What happened to our baby?" His face was pale beneath his tan.

"Shut the door!"

"I have a right to know, I'm the father! Put the truck in Park and talk to me, Marley."

"Shut. The. Door."

He slammed the door closed with enough force that the entire truck rocked. Beau stared at her through the window, drenched to the skin by the relentless rain, but it was his red-rimmed eyes that broke through her silence.

"She's dead. She was stillborn." Marley gunned the engine. Beau jerked out of the way of the extended mirror, but other than a quick, guilty glance to make sure he was still upright, she got out of there as fast as she could. Tires spinning, gravel flying, she backed out of the driveway and wished she could leave the past behind as easily as she left Beau.

She shoved the truck into first gear and took off down the narrow road, struggling to breathe, the pain so strong and so deep it could've been happening all over again. Beau was right.

Someone always remembers.

CHAPTER NINE

MARLEY ENTERED her apartment with a sigh of relief and locked the door behind her.

Thanks to the steady rain, she hadn't returned to work at the construction site, couldn't go out to work on one of her other projects and didn't have the brainpower needed to concentrate on designing. So she did the thing she hated to do most—clean.

She'd started by asking Eli and Amy to help her rearrange the display areas, both inside and out, to better showcase the merchandise either already in stock or on order for Christmas. Now the fall mums, gourds, pumpkins, straw and fodder she kept on hand for Halloween and Thanksgiving took up the covered area outside guarded by a colorful assortment of scarecrows, and the ten-foot barbed-wire-topped security fence that lined her parking lot and butted up against her building. The Christmas trees wouldn't arrive until November 1 so she had nearly a month to block off a section of the lot.

Inside the main area, they'd rearranged the various concrete statues, tools and gardening accessories, and opened up the center of the room so that she could light several trees and decorate them with gardening and nature themes. Around those she planned to market miniature John Deere tractors and wagons, and various other outside necessities and accessories that also made great gifts.

It was quite an accomplishment for the day if she thought so herself. Too bad she'd still managed to find time to think about Beau.

"You going to stand there holding up the door all evening or come in?"

Marley opened her eyes and frowned at Angel where she sat in front of drape-covered windows. "Depends. Why is there a Roadster parked in my equipment garage?"

"Do you mind?"

She shook her head. "What'd Clay do?"

"Can't you guess? Your brother doesn't know when to quit. He keeps calling and he's been by here twice. I wouldn't open the door and the last time he left, I moved my car into the garage hoping he'd think I'd left town."

Stifling a moan, Marley bent and unlaced her work boots, toeing them off and grimacing at the dirt that had coated her socks at the job site then soaked in when she was out in the rain. She pulled those off, too. "He's not going to give up, you know."

Angelique tossed a magazine aside and stood up, wrinkling her nose at the sight of Marley's filthy clothes. "Dinner's almost ready."

Her stomach growled. "I haven't eaten anything but granola bars all day. You really are an angel."

Dressed in designer slacks, a beaded tank top and heels, Angelique looked as if she'd stepped out of the pages of the magazine she'd left on the couch.

"Yeah, well, no offense, but you smell like the bad end of a gym sock. Go shower while I serve."

Marley didn't argue. She headed to the bedroom and the attached bath, and moments later stood beneath the too hot water. She tried to rid her mind of all thought and disassociate herself from Beau and the pain of the past, but couldn't. She'd lived in the depths of anger and despair for weeks after her baby's death. The only thing that had pulled her to the surface was the fear she'd wind up like her mother if she didn't snap out of it. She'd gone back to work and begged for more hours, quickly figuring out that keeping busy best dulled the wounds.

Marley's stomach growled and she knew she had to get out and face Angel. Her friend had needed to talk last night and hadn't been her usual astute self. Today, however, the inquisition was sure to begin. Ready or not.

Marley turned off the tap and stepped out onto the bath mat just as someone knocked on her apartment door. *Uh-oh.* She grabbed a towel and entered the bedroom. Angel hurried in, her eyes wide and expression indignant. "Who is the hunk and *why* didn't you tell me about him?"

Marley secured the towel tighter around her and tiptoed to the open bedroom door to shut it. "You didn't let him in, did you?"

Angel blinked at her. "Well, of course I did. Now, tell me who he is."

She didn't bother stifling her groan. "Angel—"

A soft knock sounded on the bedroom door. "Marley," Beau's voice emerged low and sexy from the other side, "don't be mad at your friend. Come out. We need to talk."

"Sounds serious," Angel murmured. "Wanna clue me in so I don't have to eavesdrop so hard?"

What to do, what to do? If Clay decided to stop by and saw a Buchanan & Son truck he'd go ballistic.

Marley opened the door and peeked out. "Say what you have to say and leave."

His gaze focused on her face, his blue eyes troubled. "Come out and let's do this right." He lifted a hand that didn't look quite steady and smoothed it over his head and neck, his Marine T-shirt straining at the seams across his broad chest in the process.

One would think the military supply their people with shirts that fit. "F-fine. Give me a few minutes." She shut the door with a quiet click and locked it to make a point. Turning, she ignored Angel's surprisingly silent presence and searched for clean clothes.

"Wow. He's the guy, isn't he?"

Nodding, Marley pulled out underwear and jeans from her dresser. A shirt from the closet. She turned her back to Angel and dressed with hands that fumbled with the hook of her bra and took four tries to snap her jeans.

"Have to say, I never thought I'd meet him."

She'd never wanted any of them to meet him. "Why would you? I certainly never wanted to see him again." She snorted. "But wouldn't you know it, here he is. Not only in South Ridge, but on the building site. What are the odds?"

Angel's perfectly plucked eyebrows rose at her tone. "What are they, indeed. Sounds sort of like, I don't now, fate playing a hand?"

Marley rolled her eyes and donned her shirt. "For a recently divorced woman, you sound awfully romantic."

"Comes easy when it's not the guy driving *me* nuts on the other side of the door." Angel walked into the bathroom and grabbed a hairbrush from the basket by the sink. "Here."

"I don't care what I look like right now."

"I do." Angel studied her, shrugging her acceptance of a black Stones shirt and snug jeans. "To have the upper hand a woman always has to look her best. Trust me."

Marley relented. She ran the brush through her hair, but left the length to hang around her shoulders to dry. She wasn't fixing it for him, and even a ponytail meant putting forth an effort. Angel had stepped into the bathroom again, but when she returned with make-up, Marley put her foot down. "*No.* I'm not trying to impress him. I don't even want to *talk* to him. I just want this o—"

"Um, I can hear you." Beau's voice carried from the other side of the door.

She smacked her hand to her forehead and groaned. "Oh, Lord, help me."

"Calm down." Angel grinned. "After everything you've said about him I had a mental image, but he actually seemed nice."

"Really? And you base this on talking to him for how long? Two *seconds?*"

"I can still hear you," Beau drawled, a smile in his voice. "Come on out, Marley."

She glared at Angel before opening the door and stepping into the living room. Beau stood by the television set, a brace on his leg and a cane in his hand.

"You really hurt yourself today, didn't you?"

"Temporary setback. It'll be good to go in no time."

Typical man. Never admit to pain. What was up with that?

"Why don't you sit down," Angel urged, taking on the role of hostess. "Would you like something to drink?"

"No, thanks."

Marley waited, watched. When guys met Angel for the first time they always reacted the same way. They looked her up and down and couldn't take their eyes off her. Then their expressions turned calculating and anyone watching could see them trying to formulate a game plan to get Angel into bed. Seconds passed, but strangely enough, Beau's eyes never left Marley's. Almost as though she were the only woman in the room.

Yeah, right. Marley crossed her arms over her chest. "What do you want?"

"I want to talk to you."

He paused, his gaze never wavering, and a part of her wanted to tell him to go ahead and look. The fact that he didn't unnerved her even more.

"Alone, if possible."

"So much for eavesdropping or sitting in." Angel

shrugged. "I'll go downstairs and see what trouble I can get into there."

"No. Angel—"

"Thanks, I'd appreciate it."

Marley shut her mouth with a snap and resigned herself to the fact that escape wasn't an option. "Please tell me you didn't park the company truck outside my door."

Angel waited for Beau's response.

His mouth lifted in a smirk. "Afraid to be seen with me?"

Neither woman said anything.

The smirk darkened into a scowl. "I drove my truck. Pop had the movers haul it here on a carrier when we relocated. There aren't any signs on the side."

"Thank God for small favors," Angel whispered on her way out the door.

Thank God, indeed. People parked in the alley all the time because there were second-floor apartments all along this section of businesses. Without the Buchanan & Son signs on the sides, no one would pay any attention. *She hoped.*

Marley nodded toward the couch for him to have a seat. Beau gingerly lowered himself onto it, the cane he used for balance gripped tight in his large hand.

"I had to come see you. To make sure you were all right after what happened today."

"You could have called."

"You hang up on me."

She smiled. "Yeah, I guess I do."

"It's also something I had to do in person. Marley, you can't say what you did today and not tell me the whole story. You know that, right?"

She did. She'd known it the moment the words came out of her mouth, but it had been too late to take them back. *Just do it and then he'll leave.* "There's not a lot left to tell. It was raining. I slipped and fell. I went to the hospital and thought everything was okay, b-but the tests came back and they told me the impact had—it was too much. They started my labor after that."

Beau shoved himself off the couch and paced across the room in angry, limping strides. "The doctor made you go through labor? They couldn't just—"

"No." Throat tight, she pulled her knees to her chest, hugging them close.

He was silent a long moment, but she could hear him breathe. Did he feel pain on her behalf?

"There's no excuse for me not being there with you. For not supporting you and taking care of you. Maybe we weren't a couple anymore, but she was still my child. *My* responsibility. I should've been there." He turned to face her, his jaw tight, eyes bloodshot and full of regret. "It means nothing now. God knows it's too late to hear me say this, but I should've been a better person, Marley. I should've been there for you and for our baby both."

She didn't move. Couldn't. Life, the Marines, something, had helped Beau grow up. The moment was bittersweet because she found herself liking the man he'd become, the one able to stand before her and speak with such heartfelt sincerity and compassion. Too little too late, as he'd said, but true.

The pain in her heart eased, soothed by the knowledge that maybe she hadn't been such a bad judge of character after all. Maybe Beau had panicked after she'd told him he was going to be a father. She'd certainly panicked after finding out she was going to have a baby.

And maybe Clay was right.

People deserved second chances if they were genuine in their desire to make amends. Nothing could be done to change the past, but everyone knew forgiveness worked both ways. To get it, she had to give it.

"Marley, I have no right to ask, but…go back further. Before the baby. What happened between us?"

Angelique's outraged screech filtered up from within the stairwell and ended whatever response she was about to make. Multiple footsteps pounded up the steps, then the apartment door burst open and crashed into the wall with enough force to put the knob through it.

Marley gaped. "Clay, what on earth—"

Her brother didn't stop. He crossed the room in a split second, grabbed Beau by his shirt and slammed him against the closest wall. "Nice to finally meet you." He muttered the words between his gritted teeth. "You and I are long overdue for a talk, Buchanan."

Beau managed to break her brother's hold, but Clay used the opportunity to slug Beau.

Marley grabbed hold of his arm before he could manage a second. "Clay, stop! Stop it!"

Beau let out an angry roar and shoved Clay backward, far enough to get a punch in himself. Neither of them listened to her and, not knowing what else to do, Marley pushed her way between the two men so they couldn't get each other without hitting her.

"Get out of the way, Mar."

"This is between your brother and me," Beau growled, his hot breath hitting the side of her face and ear.

She shivered, hated the telling response, and prayed no one noticed. "I said, stop! Beau's injured! It's not even a fair fight!" Marley elbowed Clay in the ribs when they continued to struggle, drawing a grunt of pain from her brother. *"Stop it!"*

The men paused, glared at each other for a long moment, then released each other.

Marley was afraid to breathe wrong. "Beau, are you all right?"

"You're asking him? He's—"

"Injured!"

"Fine."

She didn't know who to be angrier at. Beau for refusing to admit he was hurt in the first place, or Clay because...he was Clay. "Then you should go."

Beau's cheek had already started to swell, his angular jaw puffing up. His gaze held hers, soft and warm with all they'd shared whether he remembered it or not. "Will you think about what I said?"

"You say another word to her and I'll—"

"I will." She tried to smile but couldn't. What a mess. "Just go. Please," she added when she saw Clay's smug expression.

Her brother's face reddened. "There you go again. Why are you saying please to him? He should be on his hands and knees—"

"Hush!" She elbowed Clay again.

Beau stared down at her and something passed between them. An understanding. Indescribable but…meaningful.

"Leave, Buchanan, otherwise I'll take you out myself and we'll finish this outside."

Marley closed her eyes and groaned. "Will you just shut up? The last thing we need is for the editor of the *South Ridge Sentinel* to be charged with beating up an injured war veteran. Beau, *go*. Clay's leaving, too, but not until after I know you've gone and aren't duking it out in the alley."

Without another word, Beau left the apartment. Marley pressed her palms to her forehead and focused on not breaking down. This was exactly what she didn't want to happen. Exactly what she was afraid *would* happen.

"What the hell were you thinking letting him in here?"

"I let him in." Angel lifted her chin. "And they were doing fine before you got here."

"Fine? *Fine?* The man ruined her life!"

Angel tilted her head to one side and regarded Marley with a sympathetic stare. "She doesn't look ruined to me."

Marley heard the sound of a Hemi engine turning over. A second later it faded away.

Clay ran both his hands through his hair. "You're

doing this to get back at me. You're both taking up for him just to—"

"Yeah, Clay, this is all about you." Angel snorted. "What kind of egomaniac makes what just happened about himself? You men are all alike."

"Don't stand there and compare me to your ex." Clay moved close to Angel, the words growled down into her face.

"*Guys.*" Marley couldn't take it anymore. The tension, the fighting. The blame. Most especially the guilt. A moment? She'd actually thought she and Beau had shared a *moment?* "Clay, your time's up. This is still my apartment. Get out."

"I'm not—"

"Get out!" The shrillness of her tone shocked her. She sucked in a ragged breath, her hands fisted at her sides. "Just get out."

He frowned. "Mar, come on, take it easy."

Tears she hadn't released in much too long overwhelmed her. She couldn't breathe. Her nails dug into her palms, but the pain didn't distract her. Falling apart. She felt as though she was falling apart, and she was desperate to hold herself together. The past, the baby, her mother and Beau. Having to live it all again. She wrapped her arms around her stomach.

Angel pulled her into a hug, the words she murmured distant. All she could think about was that it should've been her mother comforting her, should've been her mother who cared.

"Clay, go. She can't do this now."

Marley sensed her brother's anger and concern,

but she couldn't bring herself to speak. She was angry at him, at Beau. At the world.

The moment the door closed the dam broke and tears slipped from her eyes. Like Angel, she hated crying. She hated the sign of weakness, especially since she'd cried too many tears for Beau Buchanan already. Why was she doing this again?

"It makes you human—and you didn't cry in front of him. That makes it all okay."

Angel's words brought out a reluctant smile. When the tears had passed, Marley wiped her eyes and slowly managed to pull herself together. "What if those two idiots come back?"

"Then I tackle you so you can't jump in between them again, and we let them kill each other. At least then they'll be out of our hair."

Marley snickered, the sound thick and rough. That was such an Angel thing to say and a horrible thought, but it kind of appealed. Things would be quieter that way. Her stomach growled loudly and she welcomed the distraction. "Please tell me you have something decadently chocolate for dessert."

"What kind of a friend would I be if I didn't? Don't we always take care of each other?" Making a goofy face guaranteed to make Marley smile, Angel held up her hand, pinky finger extended. "Cradle to grave."

Marley sniffled and did the same. Their pinkies wrapped around each other, she thought of the many years they'd weathered as loyal friends, sisters and surrogate mothers all rolled into one and smiled wryly. "Friends till the end."

Angel squeezed tight before dropping her hand and wrapping her arm around Marley's shoulders. Side by side they walked toward the kitchen. "Gotta tell you, Lucy. The way our love lives are right now? I think Thelma and Louise were on to something."

CHAPTER TEN

TWO HOURS LATER Beau stood staring out the window of his shrink's office.

"I can't say that I approve of the way the information was relayed, but it is an enlightening piece of the puzzle. How did it make you feel?"

A laugh rumbled out of his chest. "You're kidding, right? How did it make me *feel?* I feel like a Class-A jerk. What kind of man does that to a woman? To his baby?"

"Sounds to me like you were still very much a kid at eighteen."

"That doesn't excuse it."

"That's a very adult way of looking at it. You came straight here from there?" The doctor waited. "Beau?"

"I had time to kill and didn't feel like going home."

"I see. So where did you go? Did you have another confrontation with Marley's brother?"

He lowered his head and pressed it against the cool glass, not caring that he probably smudged the doc's perfectly clean window. "No. I went to the park." The one he stared at now. The kids playing on the swings, giggling as they went down the slide. He hadn't paid any attention to the boys, but every little girl had caught his eye and he'd probably freaked out a few moms.

"You're mourning your daughter, aren't you?"

He nodded. "I close my eyes and it's easy to see a little girl who looks like Marley. It kills me that..." He couldn't continue. There wasn't an obscenity out there that reflected how he felt.

"It's a perfectly understandable reaction. You feel a loss any caring person would feel." The doctor shifted and put his notepad aside. "I had a busy day today, but I think we need to discuss this in detail. Have you eaten? I've learned I think a lot better on a full stomach. You're my last patient, and while this is a bit unusual, I could order something in and we can take as much time as you like to talk about this."

Beau turned to look over his shoulder at the older man. He had a professorial look to him with his beard, mustache and round-framed glasses. The gray at his temples matching the gray of his suit. He turned back to the glass. "Whatever works, Doc."

All he knew was that he didn't want to go home. For once, he was in the mood to talk.

BARRY'S LEGS COLLAPSED under him and he fell back into the old worn recliner behind him. "*What?*"

"I got her pregnant, blew her off and later the baby died." Beau watched him closely. "Be honest, Pop. You didn't know? You weren't keeping it a secret?"

He shook his head, unable to do more. A baby? *He would've been a grandfather?*

Barry opened his mouth to reassure Beau only to close it again, his chest tight. What could he say? From the sound of it, Beau knew the ramifications of what he'd done. What he'd lost by being so wild and irresponsible. "That's why her brother beat you up?"

"He got in a few lucky shots." Beau shook his head in disgust. "I can't be too mad at the guy because after hearing what I did, I deserved it."

To some extent, but he was angry on Beau's behalf. He'd had a major head injury—springing that kind of news on him could've done a lot of damage and yet the girl's brother had tried to beat him up?

"After I left her place I went to my appointment."

"And?"

Beau shrugged. "We talked. Dr. Steinman apparently didn't have a family to go home to because he ordered dinner for us and we talked it out. Why I feel guilty now, about growing up and being a different person than I was then. That sort of thing." He lifted the bag he still carried in his hand. "Here, catch. Dinner was so good I picked up some for you on the way home. Thought you might like it."

Barry caught the bag, his eyes widening when he caught a whiff of the food inside. "Fish?"

"Yeah. I'll be eating there every time I have to go see the shrink, I can tell you that."

"You ate this?" Barry stared at his son, saw him nod and sucked in an unsteady breath before he scrambled out of the recliner and hurried to the kitchen, tossing the food onto the counter.

Beau followed him. "What's wrong?"

Beginning to wheeze, Barry felt his heart racing out of control. Beau stared at him as if he'd lost his mind. Maybe he had. His son had changed due to the head injury, but no way could he change—

Fear settled in the pit of his stomach and he leaned against the countertop, his hands gripping the edge in an effort to keep himself upright.

Oh, Lord Almighty.

"Pop? Are you okay?"

Tightness filled his chest, not allowing him to catch his breath. He knew the signs, the symptoms, and fumbled in his pocket for the inhaler he kept with him, dropped it and watched dazedly as it skidded away on the linoleum. *"Lord, help me."*

"Pop, sit down. Take it easy, I'll get it."

He felt himself being led to one of the kitchen chairs. Pressed into it. Pop. *Pop?*

"Here." The inhaler appeared before his face and Barry grasped it in his shaking hands, having to use both just to have the strength to squeeze it.

"I'm going to call an ambulance."

He shook his head and took another puff, but the boy was up. Gone. On the phone to 9-1-1. Another pull of the inhaler. Nothing was happening. Maybe a hospital would be good. *"Beau."*

"Yeah, Pop? What do you need? I'm right here."

Barry stared into the face watching him with such concern, taking in every detail, looking closely, so closely. Until he saw the truth. Tears filled his eyes. Shaking, his chest squeezed tighter, clamping down on lungs that refused to work, his heart unable to believe what his mind now recognized. "Beau."

Everything faded to black.

THE NEXT MORNING Marley was hard at work at the construction site, but her thoughts were focused entirely on Beau and Clay. Her brother had returned to the apartment an hour later, but Angel had refused to open the door, stating that they were both fine and needed some "girl time."

Clay had eventually given in and left, and after a heart-to-heart about what they both wished they could have out of life, she'd gone to bed. Angel had stayed up, watching television with a thoughtful frown on her face.

Marley hated herself for wondering what had happened to Beau. Hated that smidgen of disappointment she didn't want to acknowledge because he hadn't returned to the apartment last night, too. She didn't want to care that Beau hadn't come back.

But there was a reason Beau's father wasn't telling him details about his life. What if the news of the baby had caused him to have a setback? Should she call and check on him?

No, no. No!

What was she doing? Thinking? Unbidden, she slid a glance over her shoulder to the house across the street and groaned. She'd left Eli in charge of the shop so she could spend the morning at the development catching up with work, and what was she doing?

She shook her head at herself. She shouldn't be thinking about Beau at all, not after what he'd done to her. She wouldn't be, either, if the changes in him weren't so drastic. Apologies, bone-melting glances that turned seconds into hours.

Head injuries were dangerous, but how could they change someone so much?

The mental battle raged on and just as she was about to toss her rake aside and grab her cell phone from her pocket, a low rumble reached her ears. The diesel truck? Seconds later the red crew cab pulled into the drive next door and Beau got out, cane and all. He'd driven there like that? The bandage was on his left leg and not his right and he'd driven himself to the apartment last night, but…

Beau had a black eye. So bruised she could see it from across the road and… Was he limping worse than before? On her way out of town she'd seen Clay walking into his newspaper office and he'd had a dark bruise by his mouth and a few puffy spots, but he didn't look that much worse for wear. How dare he pick a fight with an already injured man?

Stepping over the rake, she ignored the voice in her head telling her to leave well enough alone and started across the street. Beau saw her walking toward him and met her in the middle of the rough gravel road.

"Are you okay?"

One corner of his mouth lifted in a painful-looking half smile. He nodded. "I was going to ask you the same thing."

"I'm not the one bruised and limping. I'm fine."

"Your brother got a couple sucker punches in, that's all. And I guarantee he's hurting some, too."

Satisfaction rang in his tone and she shook her head at the statement, a small part of her hoping Clay was hurting for taking unfair advantage. "I'm sorry he attacked you."

"I'm sorry we didn't get to finish our conversation."

"What else was there to say?" She glanced at the cab of the truck. "Your dad isn't with you?"

"He's at home resting. He had an asthma attack last night and blacked out. They kept him at the hospital for a while, but released him with orders to rest. They said stress and fatigue caused it."

"He must be very worried about you to have gotten so run-down." She was struggling to breathe normally because of what the look in his eyes did to her insides.

"I told him about the baby. That didn't help."

Could it really have come as that much of a surprise? She'd thought Beau's father would have already known about the baby, that Beau would've told him when it happened. *The way you told your parents?* "He took it badly?"

"Yeah. He said he didn't know. That I'd never said anything. Then he started wheezing and the attack kicked into full gear." Beau shifted from foot to foot. "Marley, don't take this the wrong way, but you told me, right? You're not—"

"Lying?" She stiffened, straightening her shoulders. "No, Beau, I'm not. Lying was your expertise back then. I told you I was pregnant, you wanted nothing to do with me or the baby, and that was that. Don't try to turn this around on me because you're feeling guilty."

"I'm sorry." He ran a hand over his short hair. "Things were confusing enough before that was added in."

He spoke with such sadness, she faltered. "Well, it's in the past now and it's over. Your dad will feel better soon. There's no need to dwell on it." Beau didn't look convinced, but who could blame him? It probably wouldn't be over for him until he could actually remember it.

"Marley, I can't blame you for being upset with me about this. I'm mad as hell that I can't remember things I know I should. I can't even blame your brother for tearing into me because the guy wants to protect you and I understand why. I get that, I deserved this—" he motioned toward his face "—and a lot more for hurting you. But I am sorry. There's no excuse for treating you the way I did. All I can do now is apologize and be thankful that I'm not the same guy I was back then. If the situation were to happen now—"

"It most certainly wouldn't happen now. I'm not eighteen and gullible anymore."

He hesitated. "I just wanted to say I'd handle it differently."

Was that supposed to make her feel better? *Sorry I didn't care about you back then but hey, if you'd waited a while, maybe I could've.*

"Marley, you have every right to hate me. I wish there was some way I could change things, but we can't go back. Now more than ever I'd really like to get that clean slate with you."

Biting her inner lip, she was afraid to let her hopes rise. "Maybe we can, but there's only one way that could happen."

"How?"

She dug deep for strength and hardened her heart at the excited glimmer she saw in his eyes. "By proving to me that you regret the hurt you caused. Go back to Cincinnati, Beau. Go back and stay there, and let your dad and his men handle this job."

His head dropped, the glimmer fading fast. A rough, husky laugh emerged from his chest. "Careful or I'll think you hate me enough to want to be rid of me."

Why did he act as though her words hurt him? *Why did she care if they did?* "Beau, I'm not the only one affected by your presence here. You saw Clay last night. South Ridge is small and the number one pastime is gossip. You'd do us all a favor if you left."

"I can't." He lifted a hand toward the house. "I have a couple hours at best that I can work before Pop wakes up. We're behind schedule and I need to take on more of the load, not leave when he needs me."

"You did before."

His jaw firmed. "I'll always regret that I put that look in your eyes. But I'm not abandoning Pop when he needs me. I have some making up to do with him, too."

She stared up at him, growing angrier because of the tender way he said that, the way he referred to his father with such respect. One day she'd been a carefree teenager out to conquer the world, and the next a terrified one facing motherhood and a family shamed beyond measure. Beau hadn't even considered doing the honorable thing back then. He'd laughed at her tears. *What changed?*

"You've made it clear that I'm the last person you want to talk to, Marley, but I'm not going anywhere. Pop can't handle things on his own. He's tired, but as stubborn as ever and determined to look out for me, and the last few weeks—the last couple of *years*—have taken a toll on him. That's my fault. I know, I hurt you and should've been there for you and the baby, but it's too late for me to do anything about that now. It's not too late to make it up to Pop. Marley, he's taken care of me, raised me and seen me through some rough stuff. Now I need to do the same for him, and I can't do that if I leave town because you and your family don't like me."

"It's way more complicated than me not *liking* you."

His blue eyes narrowed. "What do you mean?"

Her head started to ache from the bright sun and she fished for her sunglasses, taking her cell phone out of her pocket and finding the glasses farther down in the deep cargo pants. She put the glasses on her nose, thankful for the relief they brought after a sleepless night. "The summer we met was a big deal to me. It was the first time I'd ever been away from home and on my own, and everyone in town *knew.* That trip was meant to let me dip my toes in the water before I jumped in and left home for college. Instead it was the end of college and…a lot more."

"How'd we meet?"

This was so not how she'd pictured her day, reminiscing with the man who'd blessed and ruined her life in the same act. "You were hanging out with some guys in a mall, I was visiting my grandmother and… Forget it, the rest doesn't matter."

"How long were we together?"

She stared at her feet. "Not long. A couple weeks." Sixteen days to be exact. A whirlwind tornado of quick meets, few words and sex with a guy she barely knew. Not exactly something to write home to Mom and Dad.

"So we dated and…"

She shook her head and forced a smile. "Then we were over."

He blinked at her, his expression somewhat doubtful that was possible. "Just like that?"

"Just like that. It wasn't a winter dance or prom kind of thing, Beau."

"What was it then?"

Uncomfortable, she toed the rock in front of her. "I don't know. More…more like the back of the bleachers and riding without a helmet kind of thing. The kind that fizzled fast when you'd had your fun." Sighing, she looked up and noted the rich black cast of his hair, the crease at the side of his mouth and the shadowy bristle he'd forgotten to shave off that morning. *Things she shouldn't be noticing.* "It was— It was fast and *stupid,* which explains perfectly well why it didn't last."

How weird was this, discussing one of the most painful times of her life with the man who'd caused it, all the while aware of the fact he didn't remember it?

"What did I do when you told me you were pregnant?"

Thankful she'd donned the glasses, Marley frowned, hoping he couldn't see the hurt and pain she still felt at being used and shoved aside so easily. "By then you'd already moved on. It was the end of summer, and you were dating someone else. Several people actually. You told me it wasn't your fault, that we weren't exclusive and it had been fun, and that you'd give me money if I wanted to get rid of it. Otherwise, you were sorry and that was that."

Beau paced away from her, his limping stride angry and agitated, his jaw locked. "I can't believe I was such a—Marley, I'm sorry."

"So you've said. But like *I* said, what we had wasn't much. That just proved it."

"You were better off without me. You realize that, right?"

He admitted it?

As though too agitated to stand still, Beau paced again, his cane hitting the driveway in sharp stabs. She could practically see his mind working it all through. How was it possible he'd said those words to her then and yet seemed to find them so reprehensible now?

"I should've protected you and the baby from all of that. I should've been man enough to take responsibility for my actions. I should've... I should've been there for you, *both* of you. You shouldn't have had to face your family and the gossips alone."

She agreed. But he hadn't been, nor had he wanted to be and that was of his own choosing, she reminded herself. A head injury couldn't change that.

"What else happened?" He stopped when he neared her, impatience crossing his face. "Something else happened. I see it every time we talk. Was it something with me, or when you came back here? You're not saying something, what was it? *Tell me.*"

Why not? It wasn't as if it was a secret in town. She inhaled. "Something else did happen. W-when I got back here I was in shock. I kept the pregnancy a secret for a long time. I could because it was getting cooler and I wasn't very big and… I didn't know what to do. Sweatshirts hid the bulge, though, so I thought I was safe until I figured things out. Angel helped me, but then…someone found out and then everyone knew."

She smiled briefly. "Clay was furious. He came after you much like he did yesterday. He went to the mall where we'd hung out and talked to some of your friends, tried to track you down. He was so mad when he couldn't, he hit a bar, got in a fight and Dad had to bail him out of jail." She made a face. "I was blamed for that, too. They were all mortified…so ashamed." She pushed her sunglasses up on her nose. "My dad was thinking of running for Judge in the next election, but between my getting pregnant and his son winding up in jail, he couldn't. I'd ruined everything. *Every*thing. And if that wasn't enough my mother… She ended up having a nervous breakdown." She laughed, the sound bitter. "Can you imagine? I drove my own mother over the edge. You've gotta admit, it was an incredible amount of damage for the few short weeks we knew each other."

Beau stared at her, visibly shocked. "You mean to tell me your mom—"

"Couldn't handle it." Her smile turned into a grimace. "She couldn't handle any of it. My mother spent weeks in an institution. And when she came home it was a full two years before she spoke to me again. We're still not… I don't think things will ever be the same between us."

"It was an accident, Marley. Surely she knew what happened wasn't done on purpose?"

She picked at the mud caked on her carpenter pants. "You're not getting it. I attended church with them every Sunday since I was born. I was taught better. I *knew* better. Sex without love is nothing, and that was exactly what it was—nothing. I ruined everything good in my life for a quick ride with you and when it was over, you kicked me to the curb. If it had just been me…but it wasn't. The baby was taken out of the equation, but my mom has never been the same since and it's my fault."

Beau swore.

"Please, at least tell me you understand why it *would* be best if you left. My mother isn't much better now than she was five years ago, Beau, and if she hears that you're here…"

Beau's gorgeous, blue eyes were intense, soft with kindness and concern, but hot with determination and focus. “Marley, I get what you’re saying, but I can’t leave Pop here to do this job alone. He’s given up a lot for me. You want me treating him the way I did you? I’m sorry my presence here might cause you problems, but I’m not going to leave because of a little gossip over something that happened a long time ago.”

“It’s more than a little gossip!”

“If your brother and friend keep their mouths shut, who’s going to know I’m here? I’ll lie low, work and leave when Pop does, but until then all I can say is that I won’t deliberately cause you any trouble. I promise you that, I *owe* you that.”

“You owe me more than that, you owe me *peace*.”

“Maybe I do. God knows, I regret that I treated you the way I did, but people change, Marley. I know it because I’m not that person anymore.” His gaze fastened on hers with unerring accuracy despite the glasses. “I might not remember much, but I know I’m not the kind of guy who walks away from my responsibilities now. I’m not leaving. You’re going to have to deal with that.”

CHAPTER ELEVEN

CLAY'S WORDS about second chances repeated themselves in her head the entire afternoon, echoed by Beau's. She understood wanting a new start because she wanted one for herself. What about turning the other cheek? If she thought her brother deserved a second chance after hurting Angel the way he had, if she thought *she* deserved another chance with her mother, could she really deny Beau his chance at redemption?

Being young and stupid went both ways. Could it be time to forgive and forget and move on?

Over the course of the day she saw Beau several times. Each time their eyes met, he either smiled, nodded or made some kind of comment.

Hot enough?

That design is lookin' good.

Need some help?

The statements were friendly, casual. His attempt at easing the tension and strain between them after their conversation. Surprisingly, it was working. She wouldn't have thought it possible to feel anything for Beau but anger, and she would've given anything to have met the new, conked-on-the-head Beau first. He was the man she'd seen the potential for in the boy she'd known, the one squandering his abilities by partying his way through life or at least the two weeks they'd been acquainted.

Marley got to her feet and headed toward her flatbed truck for another ornamental tree. The small-leaved Japanese maple she'd carted to the site was just the thing to finish the landscaping around the back of the house. The planting beds had been mounded and raised, using topsoil that had been trucked in and the dirt misplaced from the construction.

She didn't like adding fertilizer to the soil, that way the roots would spread, seeking out the natural foods from the surrounding soil versus binding up trying to stay close to the man-added nutrients. Once the planting was completed, she and Eli could sow the grass, spread the straw and move on to the house next door. And given the weather forecast for the week, she didn't have any time to waste. She liked having Eli around for the dirt moving and heavy lifting, but the planting she liked to do herself. She'd left Amy and Eli to cover the garden center. The eighteen-year old was a natural at talking to whoever pulled onto the lot, something Marley still struggled to do depending on their acquaintance with her parents.

Marley scooted the container to the edge only to pause when Beau called her name.

"Wait up." Wearing a frown, he hurried across the road as fast as his limping stride would carry him.

"Something wrong?" After his alpha male "you'll

have to deal with it" statement about staying in town, she hoped this wasn't a continuation of that conversation.

"You shouldn't be lifting that by yourself. It weighs more than you do."

"Not quite." But Beau didn't budge. Marley sighed and nodded, letting him help her lift the heavy tree off the bed and carry it the five or so feet to where she'd dug a hole.

"Are all the houses going to be landscaped like this one?"

Concentrating on where she walked, she shook her head. "No, this one just sold. The owner's contacted me about planting the back, as well. The rest of the houses will have a basic design that can be added to later, but right now the developer just wants them pretty enough to sell."

They set the tree down, but when she raised her head, she discovered him a scant few inches away. And her mind decided the new and improved Beau was proving to be much too appealing.

Both of them froze. Her heart thumped hard in her chest. A wild, out-of-control rhythm that matched the chaos tumbling through her head. Warnings, curiosity, need, threats from her conscience asking what was she doing. Why didn't she move? Step back?

Beau lifted a hand to her cheek and brushed away a tendril of hair. The rough pad of his thumb sent shivers through her and the not-nice part of her knew she didn't *move* because she couldn't.

Her gaze slid to his mouth and she stared, transfixed, as Beau slowly lowered his head. He gave her plenty of time to pull back. To protest. But she didn't. Why didn't—

His lips brushed hers, the softest, barest of touches that had her breath catching in her chest and a moan rising up in her throat. It wasn't just his physical changes that drew her, it was… It was this, as well. Heady, powerful feelings that emerged from the depths and coursed through her. Confused her.

"Marley."

That was all he said, her name, a whispered breath of sound, before Beau firmed the kiss and touched his tongue to her lips, sweeping into her mouth with a possessive stroke she couldn't deny. The taste of him was of hot, rich coffee and a sweetness she couldn't name.

Beau's hand slid from her shoulder to the base of her neck, into her hair, cradling her head gently and angling it. Pressing deeper, stroking, making her heart race.

A sound intruded on the quiet. She frowned, not wanting to acknowledge it, but when the crunch of tires on the gravel leading toward the houses penetrated the sensual daze Beau had created, she jerked away from him as quickly as possible and turned, moaning. Through the trees she spotted her father's pristine white sedan crawling over the rough road at a whopping two miles an hour.

Marley lifted trembling fingers to her mouth and wiped, but knew it wouldn't undo the damage she'd just allowed to happen. Had her father seen them? Surely not. The drive was lined with trees, the foliage still thick although the leaves had started to fall. Her father was no doubt concentrating on maneuvering the expensive car over the rutted road, not looking for—

What had she done?

Horrified, she watched as her dad pulled in behind her truck and stopped. The windshield separating them no barrier against the naked fury appearing on her father's face the moment he saw Beau standing so close. He knew. She wasn't sure how, but he *knew.*

"You should go."

Beau's attention shifted from her father to her. "Why?"

Her dad got out of the car wearing his most threatening prosecutor's glare. "Get away from my daughter."

Marley swallowed back a gulp of panic. "That's why," she whispered.

FIVE MINUTES LATER Beau stood in the window of the house across the street and watched as Marley argued with her dad. The man was dressed in suit slacks and a heavily pressed white dress shirt, his tie tack sparkling in the sunlight. The guy defined uptight from the top of his carefully styled hair to his spit-shined shoes.

Father and daughter both made frustrated gestures with their hands, and neither looked anywhere close to backing down. He shouldn't have left. But after slamming the car door shut and stalking toward her, Mr. Pierce had ignored Marley's attempts at civility and inane introductions and demanded to speak to her alone.

When Beau didn't move, Marley asked him to go, as well, her voice trembling and painfully embarrassed. Embarrassed of him, *them.* But of course she would be. He'd stared into Marley's eyes, hoping to show her his support in facing her parent, the same support he'd neglected to give her before.

Even now her "Beau, please just go," rang in his ears and he hated the problems he'd caused her, wanted to fix them, not make them worse by kissing her.

But the kiss had been hot and sexy and everything he'd thought it would be. Problem was he wanted more, and that wasn't going to happen. Any headway he might have made with her was now obliterated by her father's furious presence.

Beau lifted his fist and banged it gently on the wall, his gaze locked on Marley's face. He had to think of a way to change things. Repair the damage he'd caused. But until he did, he had to get to work and take some of the pressure off his pop.

BARRY STARED UP at the bedroom ceiling, tears trickling out of his eyes. Exhaustion pressed down on him and as badly as he wanted to succumb to it, he couldn't. It didn't matter how many times he wiped the tears away, they kept coming, the weight in his heart heavier and harder to bear with each one.

How could this happen? How?

He'd spent most of the evening in the hospital getting breathing treatments and shots. The meds had helped ease his symptoms and stopped his allergic reaction to the fish.

Normally he wouldn't have reacted without eating

it or coming into direct contact with the oils, but the allergy doc said that the air on the plane and the dust from the job site had combined with his neglect. The scent alone had sent him over the edge into a full-blown attack.

Still, the treatments had done nothing for the real horror that had caused the problem. Finding out that Beau wasn't really Beau…

How? How could something like this happen?

He'd stayed up all night, his body reacting to the medication as if they'd shot a fifty-cup jolt of coffee straight into his veins. It had given him plenty of time to think. To remember. To realize what he should've known all along.

A rough sob shook his frame and, knowing he was home alone, he didn't try to stop it. The bed shook as he covered his face with his arms and let the tears come, crying like he hadn't cried in years—not since Beau's mother had died. Raw cries tore out of his chest and before long the pillow beneath his head was soggy. Beau's mother and now *his son?*

What had he done to deserve to lose them both?

He'd seen something like this on a news report once about a couple of college kids getting mixed up at the scene of an accident, but who would ever think it could happen again? And in the military?

Barry rolled over in the bed. The picture of him and Beau he'd left lying on his chest falling onto the mattress beside him. His son. His *son.* Gone.

Regrets filled him. All the words he should've said but hadn't. Everyone always thought they'd have time.

An explosion. A mistake. His time with his son gone—just like that.

Thank God he and Beau had mended things some a while back. That didn't make it any easier to accept, but it helped and he owed it all to…

The boy he'd brought home from Germany.

Barry wiped his eyes and tried to decide what to do. Nothing could fix this. Nothing except doing the right thing now that the worst had happened. He had to honor Beau's memory.

"I CAN'T *MAKE* HIM LEAVE, Dad. You of all people should understand the consequences of breaking a contract."

"Then break yours," her father growled. "I'll talk to the developer and get you out of it. This is too big a job for a business as small as yours anyway."

Nothing like having your family's support. Marley lifted her chin high and fisted her hands to keep from opening her mouth and saying something she shouldn't. Her dad meant well, he loved her and she knew it, but she wasn't a child anymore, and she refused to be ordered around like one. "I'm handling this job just fine, thank you, and I will *not* break my contract."

"Only a fool gets bitten twice."

"Exactly." She'd do well to remember that, too. *She'd kissed him.* "What does it matter if he works across the street?"

"He wasn't across the street when I pulled in, he was over here and very, very close to you. What did he do?"

"Nothing! He helped me carry a *tree,* he wasn't

feeling me up!" She clamped a hand over her mouth and winced, unable to believe she'd just said that to her very prudish father. *Oh, Lord help her.* Beau's kiss really had rattled her. She hadn't wanted to outright lie to her dad but—

Dads weren't meant to know everything.

"I see. But that doesn't excuse what he did to your brother. What about him, Marley?"

"Clay threw the first punch. He brought it on himself."

"Have you stopped to ask yourself *why* he threw the first punch?"

She dropped her head, hoping to hide her hot face long enough to get control of herself.

"Do you remember how long it took before your mother could raise her head in public? *Do you?*"

"Yes! I remember perfectly well, but you don't—"

"Do you remember how long she laid in bed and cried? What about the night we had to call an ambulance to come get her to take her to the *mental* ward?" He growled the words, his voice getting lower, more intense.

She remembered it all and he knew it. But the guilt that came with what he said—loads of it, tons of it, slammed into her, forced her head lower.

She remembered it. And standing there being berated by her father made her feel very much like an eighteen-year-old kid again. A whore in her father's eyes because the boy she'd known two short weeks had gotten her pregnant. How could his own daughter sleep with a stranger? That was something only whores did, according to him. No amount of apologizing or explaining or—or *anything* had changed his attitude. Over time it had softened, the words shoved aside in light of her mother's illness, but his disapproval was always there. "I remember it all. But that was years ago and I've grown up. I made a mistake, but I learned from it and I refuse to live in the past the way Mama does."

"Don't talk about your mother that way. Of all the people in this mess, she's the innocent one."

"Is she?" Old pain combined with new. "Innocent people don't hide away from the world when they've done nothing wrong."

"That is enough! I am still your father and I'm looking out for your best interests. Working here with him is *not* in your best interests and I intend to do something about it."

"Dad, come on! You can't make me break my contract. I'm twenty-four years old. I own my own business and I'm doing very well."

"You're scraping by."

"I pay my bills and I'm in the black, that's more than scraping by. Besides, it's a big, wide world out there. Are you going to tell me you don't work with people you don't like? People you don't trust? Of course you do! You have to, but you keep an even more watchful eye on them, don't you?"

"There is a vast difference, Marley, and you know it." Her father took her elbow in hand and pulled her around to the side of the house into a foot-wide band of shade. Sweat ran down his face and glistened beneath the dark red hair she'd inherited from him. "You pay your bills, but you're working yourself into the ground and for what?"

"Hard work never hurt anyone."

"No, but the root of the problem remains. Do you remember when you used to help your mother in the garden?"

Marley blinked at him. Huh? "What does that have to do with anything?"

"You did it to make her happy. Because she liked it and you knew it made her happy. You wanted her approval to help make up for the way you two fought. What do you think this is?" he asked, indicating her truck and the landscaping nearby. "Hiring on at The Treehouse before Rickers sold out to you was just another way of trying to get her approval after *that man* destroyed our lives. You were—*are*—desperate to make your mother happy again after breaking her heart."

She shook her head. "You're reading more into this than there is. I know plants, I like being outside. And I'm good at design. My profession was an easy choice to make."

"Maybe so. But if that's the case, why destroy all your hard work by letting that—*that* back into your life?"

"We were just talking." She hoped her father would overlook the telltale heat in her cheeks or else blame it on the sun.

"There's no need for you to talk to him. He hurt you, he abandoned you *and* his baby, he broke your mother's spirit and he cost this family more than he'll ever be able to repay. You think I'm going to forget that? That any one of us can forget that? If you allow Beau Buchanan to get within shouting distance of you, it's too close, Marley. I would've thought you'd realize that."

A rough laugh escaped her. "He's just *working* here. And—whatever happened to turning the other cheek? We were young, Dad, and we made a mistake. Can't it ever be over?"

Her father's gaze narrowed. "God wants us to be forgiving, not fools. If you behave like you did back then, if you get taken in and act the wild child again, do not expect your mother and me to welcome you back a second time. As you said you are not eighteen anymore and only—"

"Fools get bitten twice," she whispered, repeating the words in her head for good measure. Getting pregnant wasn't the worst thing that had happened. No, it was the way she'd gotten pregnant, then the fall and her mother's breakdown. Those were the things she hadn't been able to overcome. Would probably never overcome.

"I'm sorry."

Her father nodded once, the move sharp, pointed. His gaze angry, but tinged with sadness and pain.

"I've got to get back to town. I have a school-board meeting in an hour. Marley, you are my daughter, and I love you. But I'm telling you now, don't do this to us again." He turned on his heel to walk away, but stopped after two steps. "This morning your mother mentioned having Sunday dinner. One o'clock."

"I—I have a lot of work to do."

"The work can wait an hour or two. And it's Sunday. You haven't been to church in a while."

She barely stopped the frown pulling at her lips. "Do you really want me there? The last time I went, Mama wouldn't even look at me."

Her father didn't comment on that. "I think you need to come, to dinner if nothing else. Maybe sitting across the table from the people who love you will remind you of the damage caused the last time Beau Buchanan *talked* to you."

Marley watched her father climb into his car and pull away. When she couldn't see him, she walked around the back of the house, hoping the shade there would help cool the heat in her body. It didn't.

What had she done? She'd kissed him. *Kissed* him! Not a sweet kiss on the cheek but a—

Shame and guilt and anger pulsed through her, surges of energizing emotions that had her dropping to her hands and knees with a moan and grabbing a hand shovel. Frantic, she began pounding it into the freshly tilled soil, pausing only long enough to yank rocks and roots out of the way. Working as fast as she could to get the bad stuff out so that the good could grow.

Clay wouldn't have told a soul that Beau was there. Her father wouldn't have known had he not seen Clay and demanded to know about the fight, but who knew what conclusions people would jump to when they saw Clay? If someone mentioned the scene when she'd first talked with Beau, just the mention of his name with hers could have rumors spreading like wildfire.

"Marley?" Without warning, Beau knelt beside her.

She shook her head and ignored him completely, focusing on the task in front of her. No one was going to keep her from proving to her parents, the town and *Beau* that she wasn't the same girl she'd been. She wasn't naive anymore, wasn't gullible or out to prove the good girl could be bad. How stupid was that? How immature? She'd thought she knew so much, but now she knew better. She wasn't going to be taken in by Beau's beautiful eyes and sinful smile.

He put his hand on her back, the touch light, gentle. Startling her nonetheless.

"Marley? Honey, take it easy. You're going to hurt yourself if you keep at it like that. What did he say to you?"

"What do you think?" She panted, breathing heavily from her frantic digging, every stab of the shovel harder than the last. "I'm sorry, Beau. You might have changed—Lord knows I hope you *have* because if it's true then you won't treat any other woman the way you treated me, but—" She shook her head and her ponytail caught at the corner of her mouth, a reminder of how he'd brushed the tendril away and… "Go away. Please, I want you to *go away.*"

"Marley—"

She jerked her head up, meeting his gaze dead-on. "I chose you over them once, Beau, and look what happened. Now it's all blowing up in my face—*again*—because you're here. If you've changed, great. Fantastic! But if you meant what you said about wanting a clean slate—now's the time because I want one, too. I want one *here,* in my hometown, and you being in the picture is ruining everything for me."

"I'm sorry. I know it takes time for people to forgive and forget."

A near-hysterical laugh bubbled out of her mouth. It was horrible to think, to believe, but some so-called good people were the very first to judge. To condemn. Forgive and forget? That seemed impossible to achieve. How many times did a person have to say she was sorry?

How many times has Beau said he's sorry to you? Is it enough?

"It takes more than time, Beau." She indicated the dirt in front of her. "Look at this. Do you see this? To get something to grow here I've got to get rid of all the—the bad stuff that'll keep it from happening. The same is true for me, for my life. I need rid of the bad stuff and—"

"I'm the bad stuff," he acknowledged, his voice low and gravelly and sounding more than a little hurt.

Pain pierced her. She wasn't a mean person. Unlike her mother and her friends, she tried to keep an open mind. To not gossip or cause others pain because she'd been on the receiving end. She didn't want to hurt Beau but… After a moment's hesitation, she nodded. "You're the bad stuff."

CHAPTER TWELVE

"GET YOUR SHOES ON, DORK. We're going to get something to eat and get away from the bad stuff Pop's been cookin'."

"Where are we going?" He looked up and saw a boy leaning against the doorway. The kid had long black hair and was tall and lanky, too thin for his size.

"Does it matter? At least it's not Pop's. Boy, I can't wait for Mom to come home from Aunt Ginny's. Come on. I call the front seat."

He tossed the He-Man figure aside and scrambled to his feet. "But it's my turn!"

The kid rolled his eyes and gave him a glare. "I'll give you a head start, but first one to get there, gets it. Don't be stickin' your head out the window like a dog if you win, though. Somebody might see."

He grabbed his shoes and pulled them on, forgoing the laces. "Hey, Joe, you think Pop will take us huntin' for crawdads? He knows how much we like them and Mom's not here to complain about the mess. Joe? Hey, wait up, Joe! That's not fair! That's my seat!"

"Hey. Hey, come on, son, wake up. Food's on.

You got about fifteen minutes to be ready to fight for your share."

Beau opened his eyes and stared up at the ceiling, the dream slowly fading away like Pop's footsteps down the hall. How could he have forgotten to ask Pop about the kid named Joe?

He lifted his hands and rubbed his bleary eyes, blaming his heavily medicated state last time for the lapse. The ever-present headache that came with the memories pounded through his temples and he winced from the pressure.

"Hey, Pop, do you know a—" Stilling, he could hardly believe it when the name formed on his lips the same time an image sprang into his mind. Full-blown, detailed, he'd know the kid if he saw him in a picture. He'd remembered something else!

"What's that?" Pop called from the opposite end of the house.

Beau hurried out of the bedroom toward the kitchen. He'd worked at the job site, come home to check on Pop and found him holed up in his room, snoring as usual. The late night and hot work had caught up with Beau so he'd decided to sleep while he could, reminding himself that he was still recovering from his own hospital stay. The last thing he wanted was for Pop to wake up raring to go while he was too tired to move.

The E.R. docs had blamed Pop's asthma attack on stress and fatigue and the grit associated with construction. He couldn't do anything about the dust and dirt, but he could certainly pitch in more now that he was out of the service and back on his feet.

His physical therapy was doing wonders and his shoulder didn't hurt that much anymore. He'd have to watch getting up and down and make sure he didn't twist the ligaments in his thigh damaged by the shrapnel, but if he was careful, he could definitely put in more hours and help his father out.

In the living room he stopped to take a look at the few picture frames scattered among the bookshelves. The moving company had not only packed them up, but using Polaroid pictures, they'd also unpacked and arranged things as close as they could to the Cincinnati house. He didn't see the kid he'd dreamed about, though.

"Lookin' for something?"

Beau nodded and moved to the last part of the three-sectioned bookcase. "I had a dream—a memory."

"What about?"

He kept looking, examining each picture closely. Most of them looked to be of him as a kid. "There was a kid named Joe. Do you remember him?"

"Son, come and eat. There's time for that later."

"Think back, Pop, are you sure? Dark hair, thin? I remember him really well. All I have to do is see a picture of him. Where's the pictures of me as a kid? Snapshots of my friends? Are they here somewhere?"

"Son—"

Beau lifted a hand and pressed it hard to his throbbing temple. Joe, Joe, *Joe*. He remembered him, it was all right there. All he had to do was get through the fog. "You've gotta remember him. We must've hung out together. I remember him a lot, like he was always around."

His father didn't so much as blink, but he looked pale and he was searching his pocket for his inhaler again.

"Pop?"

He put the plastic end in his mouth and squeezed, inhaling and closing his eyes. The wheezing continued and actually got worse.

"Hey, Pop, take it easy. Are you all right?"

His dad backed up until he leaned against the arm of the couch, his hand shaking as he used his inhaler again. Pop nodded slowly, avoiding his gaze.

"Pop, it's fine. Whatever it is. Marley told me what happened between us and I handled it okay. I won't lose it the way I did at the hospital."

"I can't." Pop shook his head. "Too dangerous."

Beau fought his frustration. "Joe was a friend, right? Did something happen to him?"

Pop pulled the puffer from his mouth, his breath rasping in and out of his chest, the dark circles under his eyes prominent. "The doctors—I don't want to hurt you. Give it time."

Disappointment crowded him, but he didn't have the guts to push things further. Not with Pop's health at stake. "Okay. It's okay, I understand."

Pop knew something about Joe, something big. But would Pop not tell him what it was because of his health? Or because Pop couldn't handle the news himself?

SUNDAY AFTERNOON Marley seated herself across the table from Clay and ignored the angry glower on his face because she hadn't been able to talk Angel into accepting his invitation to lunch.

Marley had added her request to Clay's, but Angel had said something mysterious about a business call and taking a run when she'd left, and Marley hadn't seen her since.

"Let's say grace."

They bowed their heads and her father asked God for extra support and a loving hand for his wife, guidance for those struggling to make the right decisions for the good of their family. She got the point.

Once the Amens were said, her father grabbed his bowl from the table in front of him and began spooning soup into it.

"I thought Mama was going to join us."

"She was. Now she's not."

Marley fiddled with her napkin. "I'm sorry I didn't make it to church this morning."

"It's just as well."

Okay. "Did Mama go?"

"For a while. We had to leave early."

"Why?" Clay pressed. "Something happen?" He shot Marley a quick glance.

"She got upset. The message was purity of body and thought and—"

Marley dropped her spoon and it clattered onto the plate. "And she thought of me," she finished for him.

"Parents worry about their children, Marley. No matter their age." Her father looked at her intently, then turned his attention to Clay. "You aren't a hotheaded kid anymore. We can't let that man's presence in this town get the better of us."

Us. He said that as if she wasn't one of them. "Wait

a minute, Mama knows he's here? That's why she went to bed?"

Her father nodded grimly. "I was afraid someone would tell her and thought it best she hear it from me. She went to church to seek comfort, but couldn't find it."

"So she came home and found it in her medicine. She knocked herself out again, didn't she? Beau's in town, Dad, not in my bed."

"Marley." Clay shot her a warning glare.

"That is quite enough," her father agreed.

Desperate, Marley gripped the edge of her seat and decided to speak her mind. At this point, what did she have to lose? "Why can't I speak honestly? It's just us."

"This isn't appropriate conversation for Sunday dinner."

"Yeah, well, apparently I gave up being appropriate long ago," she murmured drearily. "Look, Beau's in town and we're going to have to deal with it. All I'm wondering is why Mama has to go upstairs and take a pill. Hiding behind a closed door is one thing, but she drugs herself, too."

"Do not talk about your mother like she's—"

"An addict? Maybe she is."

Clay's eyes bugged out of his skull. *"Marley."*

"It's prescribed medication, and you're questioning why she needs it?" Her father's hand landed on the table. Dishes clattered. "How insensitive are you that you can't see the problem, Marley?"

A knot formed in her stomach. "I know I stress her. I always have, Dad, and that was back when I was just another teenage girl, but I don't live here now. Her responsibilities for raising me are over, and I'm just saying most moms talk a situation out or—or yell and get upset and then they get over it. But not Mama. She drugs herself to keep from facing reality and you both need to acknowledge that. It's getting worse."

"She's fine."

Marley couldn't hold back a laugh because Clay and her father growled the statement in unison. She pushed her plate aside. "She's not. When are you going to see her behavior for what it is? How can she get better if she can't move on? She claims to be a Christian, but what kind of Christian holds on to my mistake with both hands and—"

Her father stood up from his chair so quickly the chair fell backward, striking the antique buffet cabinet behind him and leaving a gash. "You want to discuss religion? *Really?*"

Heat rushed into her face. "I'm not perfect," she whispered. "I know that very, very well. I—I'm just saying I think Mama needs help because she's getting worse. She needs to get out of the house. She needs to do things, go see a *professional,* because drugging herself *repeatedly* certainly isn't helping."

Her father tossed his napkin onto the table. "And I think you need to look inward for the source of her pain. If you can't do that, look across the table. Your brother fought the man who used you and tossed you aside and what do you do? You defend Beau Buchanan's right to stay in town. You're sitting in my house—*my house!*—taking up for him instead of your family! You blame your mother for wanting peace from her upset and yet all you've done is cause more chaos by taking a job working with the very man who put your mother in this condition in the first place!"

"I didn't know that when I took the job! And it's not Beau's fault that Mama can't—"

"*You* blame others for their faults, but you can't see your own! You feel sympathy for other people, but not your own *family. You've* made choices you knew we wouldn't approve of, and now you're doing it all over again?"

"I'm not doing anything! I'm just trying to—" Marley broke off and watched her father stalk out of the room. Seconds later the front door slammed, and she flinched at the sound.

Clay scooted his chair back and got up, as well.

"Clay, please."

"We all make mistakes, Mar, but accusing Mom of being an addict wasn't the way to go about getting Dad to see your view. Especially not after telling him you're still going to work with Buchanan."

"I know I screwed up. Clay, how can I *not* know it? But Beau and my contract aside, all I want is to get Mom the help she needs. She's upstairs *drugged* out of her mind!" Clay looked torn between believing her and upset that she defended her position with Beau, but she pressed on. She couldn't do this by herself. "Do you think I'm to blame for all of this? For Mama?"

Jaw tight, her brother didn't quite meet her gaze. "I think we're all to blame. And I think you need to figure out a way of helping Mom without making things worse." He shook his head. "And I think that's not really possible right now, not while Buchanan is here." That said, Clay left, too.

Marley remained at the table for a long time, staring at the mess that should have been a good Sunday dinner. The kind they used to have until that fateful summer.

Trembling, she gathered up the dishes and put the unused ones back in their place and the rest in the dishwasher, desperate to busy herself and get her mind off the kiss she'd shared with Beau. Maybe she was focusing on the changes in him more than she should, but between Beau and her family right now, Beau seemed to understand her better. He'd changed. And so had she.

Marley wandered through the big, silent house, remembering better times. Christmases and birthdays, sleepovers with friends. The perfect family her parents had demanded they be up until the pressure had turned her to rebellion. The need to get out of the house, away. The need to lash out and become her own person.

Books and magazines declared the teenage years problematic for mothers and daughters. But this had been so much more. The fights, the arguments. Not being allowed to do something because her mother was afraid of what might happen. Because she was afraid of what people would say, think. Afraid to do anything but live by other people's standards and rules.

Her foot hit something and with a start, Marley looked up, the ornate staircase a showpiece of stained, hand-carved wood and perfectly painted risers. Symbol for her father's upper-middle-class family. A big, riverfront home, nice cars, the so-called perfect life. Public images upheld at all costs, any personal dirt swept under the rugs and into closets if at all possible. She'd changed that. Made their private life public because her father's running mates had harped on her pregnant state, his son's trip to jail and his wife's sad inability to cope. There were times she was surprised her father was still around. Times she was amazed that he hadn't packed up and left them all to escape the shame of it.

Marley stood at the top of the stairs. She walked down the hall to her old bedroom, nothing like the way it had when she'd lived there. Now it, too, was the image of perfection. No hint of the past or what had happened remained. Nothing to show that she'd ever been part of their lives, no scarlet letter to mark her disgrace.

Back in the hallway, her parents' bedroom door was shut. She tiptoed over, hesitated, then slipped inside the darkened interior. The shades were drawn, her mother asleep in the four-poster bed.

Frowning, Marley followed her instincts, knowing, deep down, she was right. In the attached bathroom, she opened the medicine cabinet, taken aback when she didn't find what she expected.

Where were they? She moved to the linen closet. Nothing? Could she be wrong?

Marley reentered the bedroom and crossed to her

mother's nightstand. The top drawer contained nothing but an old bestseller, lotion, lip balm. A few other odds and ends like pens and a small notebook. Her mother's Bible. *No pills.*

She leaned over the side of the bed, kissed her mother on the cheek. "Forgive me, Mama."

Marley turned to leave, but her leg caught on the edge of the bottom drawer. One of two she hadn't opened. Hesitating, feeling guilty, she slowly bent to close it. She had no right to look through her mother's things. But she couldn't stop herself. A thick throw was folded neatly and tucked behind it…

A small, pink plastic container full of little brown pharmacy bottles. Marley pulled the box from the drawer and lifted the lid.

Eight. Eight bottles inside. She made note of the names, but other than a few from commercials repeatedly playing on television, she didn't recognize them.

Blinking back tears, she repeated the names over in her head, trying to memorize them, noting that they were from three different doctors, two different pharmacies.

She ran through the names again, finally remembered the paper and pen in the top drawer and scrambled to write down the information with hands that shook.

It was up to her. She had to do what was right. For her family. *Herself.* Protect everyone involved because she hadn't done that the first time around. How many pills did it take to keep her mother away from the edge of insanity? The insanity Marley had caused?

Deep down she knew her father would never support her. He'd continue to pretend everything was fine, even if she confronted him with the evidence she held in her hands. She didn't know which of her parents was more fragile. Her mother had her pills to see her through the hard times, but her father couldn't work any harder than he already did to bury his emotions and his family's problems. It was entirely up to her to set things right and do what had to be done.

But where did she begin?

FOUR DAYS LATER Barry hesitated outside Dr. Steinman's office door, then forced himself to knock and go in.

"Mr. Buchanan, come in. My service said you were on your way to see me."

He shut the door and crossed the room to shake hands with the doc. "Thanks for working me into your schedule."

"No, problem. It's good to see you again. Have a seat. Did you enjoy the fish? Beau said he was taking some home to you."

"It was…fine."

The doctor's brows lowered as he caught on to Barry's mood. "I see. I take it this is a serious matter to have you dropping by without Beau. Did something happen? Is Beau all right?"

Barry seated himself in one of the chairs across from the doc's desk, then just as quickly jumped to his feet and strode to the window. "He's… Yeah."

"Perhaps you'd like to discuss your thoughts about

your son's condition? What it's been like dealing with Beau's amnesia?"

He nodded. "I need some advice about—about that."

"Absolutely. What's the problem?"

"He wants answers. Answers to things I can tell him, but I'm not sure if he's ready to hear it all. Important things that would upset him."

"Letting patients remember on their own or slowly is recommended for a lot of reasons, Mr. Buchanan. If there's something in particular on your mind, we have procedural ways of dealing with it. I'd be happy to speak with Beau about it during our next session. It's best if the information is layered into the conversation slowly so that I can gauge his reaction and ensure that he's able and ready to cope with the news. If it helps you, you've done the right thing by not telling him whatever it is you think would upset him."

He wasn't so sure. Barry wiped a hand over his face, smoothing it around his neck to squeeze. The boy he'd brought home from Germany would be the one to pay the price. A setback, the risk of seizures. And when the press found out—he didn't want to imagine how bad the media frenzy would be. Beau was gone and nothing would bring him back. But now it was up to Barry to make things right by protecting the boy left in his care. In the meantime he had to find out where Beau's body had been buried, and prepare to bring his son home when the truth became known.

Barry slid his hand into his pocket, holding on to his inhaler because he could feel the vise forming around his chest. He closed his eyes against the glare of the sun in the window, and reminded himself that he was fine now. Stronger. He'd had time to cope. Time to rest and come to terms with the news. He'd gone back on his medication to get his asthma under control, mourned in his dark, quiet bedroom. Now it was time to deal with facts.

"Mr. Buchanan? You made this trip for a reason. What does your son need to be told?"

His thumb rubbed the hard plastic of the inhaler. "He needs… He needs to know that he lost his best friend in the explosion." The words hurt. He hated misleading the doctor, hated lying and wanted to tell him everything, but because of the circumstances there was a good chance the doc would feel compelled to inform the authorities, and that wasn't a risk he would take. If it were Beau's mental well-being at stake, he'd want it put before everything else, including himself. "He needs to try to remember him because if he does…it would answer a lot of his questions."

"I see. Can you tell me a bit about this person? I take it he was a soldier, as well?"

Barry nodded. He should just open his mouth and tell the doc everything, but it was best this way. "They were friends and—they even looked a lot alike." Barry swung around to face the doc. "Like brothers, nearly twins. They were close, Doc, and he needs to remember him soon. The sooner, the better."

"And his friend's name?"

“Jack.” Barry swallowed the lump in his throat, pulling the inhaler from his pocket. He pulled off the tip and ignored the sting of tears in his eyes. “Master Sergeant Jack Brody.”

CHAPTER THIRTEEN

A WEEK LATER BARRY stared down at the newspaper a long time after Jack had turned pale-faced and sweaty and stalked out of the grocery store. Beside photos of the changing October foliage and recommended dishes for the upcoming Thanksgiving holiday, a separate headline read that six more American soldiers were dead. His heart ached for their parents, for the pain they'd suffer on a daily basis from this time forward. For the pain he suffered himself with every beat of his heart.

His son— His *son* had been one of those boys and he hadn't even known it.

Beau's friend was getting better. Eating more. Getting more inquisitive. It was only a matter of time before Jack remembered enough to understand why his memories didn't match the snapshots of Beau's life. Then Jack would know the truth, that he'd survived the suicide bomber while Beau had died. That somewhere along the way they'd been mixed up.

How many people resembled each other in the world? Most were blood relatives of some sort, but some weren't. Just like Jack and Beau. They'd been so similar in size and height, nearly identical to those who didn't know them well. Beau's e-mails had been full of his and Jack's pranks and practical jokes.

Side by side they'd been quite a sight, not enough to fool him or Beau's mother, but *that* close.

His thoughts returned to Jack, whether or not he should go after him or leave the boy alone and let him get some air. Dr. Steinman said he'd begin to talk to the boy about Jack at the next session. A detail here, a nudge there.

He'd worked hard to stress the differences between the two boys to the doc in the hopes of helping Jack separate himself from Beau in his mind. Begin to realize that things weren't adding up.

So far Jack's memories were of growing up. Of his brother, Joe, the one who'd gone to prison for killing his baby girl. What would happen when Jack remembered his teenage years? The time during which the murder had taken place? He wouldn't understand, would mourn the baby all over again and get upset as he rightly should. He didn't know how else to help Jack. Didn't know if he was doing the right thing.

Barry's gaze focused on the newspaper and he realized the answer was right there on the front page. The family's grief and heartache appeared in full color and sold for a mere dollar and change. But how cruel was it to let Jack's family go on believing him dead?

He'd changed his mind a million times, picked up the phone to call the doc at least once an hour since. But every time he'd hung up, knowing Jack couldn't handle that yet. He wasn't well enough. And if the media got wind of the story, every newspaper and TV station in the world would show it. Vultures waiting for a story. He couldn't do that to Jack. The boy didn't deserve it, especially not after helping Beau and Barry to find their way back to one another.

Beau had told him Jack had left town the moment he turned eighteen. How he'd begged his father to come with him, but the man had chosen a murderer over Jack. How could he push the boy into remembering a family like that?

"Excuse me. Sir?"

Barry started, then moved out of the way of the young mother pushing an overloaded cart and two kids. The woman had red hair, long and curly like Marley Pierce's.

How strange was it that Jack seemed drawn to the woman, as well? Nothing good could come of that. Especially now. Jack hadn't said much about her lately, but sometimes that said more than words could.

Barry wiped a shaking hand under his nose and went back to his shopping. God had seen him through some tough times in the past, and He'd see him through this, too. He just had to believe that this had happened for a reason. That he was supposed to help get Jack back on his feet. Thinking that, believing that, was the only way he could put one foot in front of the other and keep moving forward. He'd find out why when the time was right.

BEAU SAT UNDER A SHADE TREE outside the grocery store and took in the small town. He'd gone into the store with Pop and made it as far as the office at the front, but the farther he'd walked, the more anxious he'd felt. And then he'd seen the headlines about the soldiers who'd died and been sick in an instant, the suffocating lack of oxygen making his head whirl.

A baby had screamed from somewhere in the store and he'd turned, desperate to find it, keep it safe—only to realize the few people around who'd noticed his rapid about-face eyed him with leery looks that said they thought he was several cards short of a whole deck.

On the bench he felt fine, making him wonder if he shouldn't get his butt back inside and face the crowd, push through the gut-clenching fear and be done with it. He sat forward, his hands locked on the wooden slats beneath him, legs jelly. Go on. Do it.

"Come on, do it."

"No."

"You're going to blow my chance with her because of a few technicalities?"

He stared at the back of the guy's head and watched as he dressed in desert fatigues. "I just got off duty."

"It's not like you haven't pulled a double before. Come on, do this for me. She's a nice girl."

"Then why is she going out with you?"

"I asked myself the same question, which is why since she said yes, I don't want to blow it. They'll never know."

"Okay, whatever."

The guy pulled his arm back in a "yes!" motion. "Thanks, man. I'll make it up to you. Now, all we have to—"

A short, muffled cry sounded behind him. Jerking

out of his daze, Beau saw a blond woman stumble and fall to the ground. Marley's friend.

He hurried over to her. "Are you okay?"

Angel rubbed her ankle. "Yes."

"What happened?"

She gave him a mulish glare, her features pinched with pain. "I saw you sitting there and wanted to throw a rock at you for making Marley cry, and next thing I knew I twisted my ankle."

Beau knelt down beside her, hiding a smile when it occurred to him Marley and her friend weren't that graceful. "Sounds like your evil thoughts caught up with you. And I'm sorry I made Marley cry. Come on, let me help you up."

"I can get— *Ow*. Oh, *ow!*"

Eyeing the foot she rubbed, he winced. "That ankle's already swelling. Could be broken."

"It's not. It's just—" She looked around, a bright flush to her otherwise pale cheeks. She lifted a painted finger and pointed. "Help me over to the bench. I'll sit there until it stops hurting."

"How about I take you to a doctor instead? I think there's an urgent-care clinic around here somewhere."

"It's fine."

"You got a thing against doctors?"

"Only when they're poking at me."

"Yeah, well, that I can understand. I've had enough of that myself." He grabbed her elbow and pulled her to her feet, limping beside her until she hopped her way over to the bench. By the time they got there she was trembling and biting her lip. "Are you sure you don't want me to take you to—"

"No."

He settled her, then left long enough to cross the street.

She needed an ice pack or a bag of frozen vegetables to keep the swelling down. He eyed the grocery door momentarily. No, no way.

Outside the store were a couple of soda machines. His best option at the moment. He bought a bottle and retraced his steps, his mind crowded with questions Angel could answer about Marley since she wasn't speaking to him.

"Here." He lifted her foot, noting that she'd removed her shoe and sock, and carefully sat down on the opposite end of the bench, gently propping her foot higher by placing it on his knee. That done, he held the cold bottle against her ankle and heard her hiss of pain over the crackling of the dry leaves blowing all around them. "Sure you don't need that doctor?"

She leaned her head back and took a deep breath, eyes closed. "No, I— It's feeling better, and…thanks, okay? There, I said it. Just don't get any ideas that we're friends or anything."

"I wouldn't dream of it." He turned on the bench to face her. "Did we ever meet? Back then?"

Settling herself more comfortably, Angel blinked at him. "No—because if we had, I'd have set you straight on a few things."

He chuckled and noticed a corresponding smile on

her lips, figuring the pain of her ankle was lessening. "I don't doubt that."

"I knew the moment she called from her grandmother's house and said she'd met you that you were going to hurt her." She turned her gaze out toward the town. "I didn't grow up on Riverfront like Marley, but I saw how her parents and half the town put her on a pedestal."

"Were you disappointed in her, too?"

That earned him a glare. "I was glad she'd finally broken free of the chain around her neck and had fun for once in her life. Just sorry it had to be with you."

He winced. "And now? She won't talk to me."

"Do tigers lose their stripes?" Angel sighed and wriggled her foot without grimacing. "Marley loves what she does, but do you really think she wants to work sixteen-hour days? Whether she realizes it or not, she's trying to claw her way back up that stinking pedestal and she'll never make it. Which is why I want you to listen to me, Beau Buchanan. If you hurt Lucy again, if you ruin what little of the so-called reputation that she's managed to rebuild, Clay will be the least of your worries. Hell hath no fury like a best friend scorned."

"I understand." He nodded once. "Lucy?"

She waved a negligent hand. "Inside joke."

Beau stared at her, glad Marley had a friend like Angel to look after her. Everyone needed someone like that. Someone to see them for who they are, not what other people thought of them or wanted them to be.

"How bad was it?" he asked finally. Unable to bear the thought of Marley in pain, he locked his jaw. "When she lost the baby. How bad was it?"

Angel looked down at her hands and released a soft breath. "Bad. She was late for work and ran out of the house. It was raining. All it took was five steps. Marley was crying because her arm hurt really bad from the break. Then they checked the baby and..."

The seconds passed as they sat there, him on one end of the bench, Angel on the other, the sounds of cars and people and boats on the nearby river fading to nothing. "I can't believe they made her go through labor anyway."

"We couldn't, either, but the doctors said it was best."

"What about her mom?"

Angel's expression hardened. "Marley's fall from perpetual sainthood had sent her into depression, but she was on medication and seemed okay, but the house was like a tomb and you never knew what might set her off. While they set Marley's arm Donna was quiet, but under control. But when they came in with news about the baby... She had to be sedated. Marley needed her mom so bad right then, but Donna couldn't hold it together for her." Angel swore softly, her blue eyes glittering with tears. "That's another reason we're so close. Neither one of us have mothers we can depend on, but we know no matter what, we've got each other. We're each other's family, sisters by choice."

He didn't know what it was about her words, but they struck a chord in him. "It's no wonder Marley's family hates me so much. I can't blame them after hearing everything Marley went through."

"We all hated you for a while," Angel whispered huskily. "We hated you for treating Marley that way and not caring. She wasn't the same after that. She grew up instantly and not in a healthy way. It was too much, too fast. Anyway, Donna lost it. And I don't mean she got upset, but that she literally lost it."

"Marley told me."

"She blames herself. All her life her parents practically had her locked in a chastity belt. So strict she wasn't allowed to do anything and when she did get a little freedom look what happened."

He turned the bottle to a cooler side against her ankle, watching a drop of condensation trickle down onto her skin. "Are you the same person you were five years ago?"

"Oh, please. Don't turn all psychoanalytical on me. Buttering me up won't help you with her family, trust me. I'm hated nearly as much as you." She grinned as though proud of the fact. "I gave Marley her first drink of *devil water*."

The description had him smiling. "That's bad, but not as bad as getting her pregnant."

She relented with a shrug. "True enough. You win."

He definitely hadn't won. "Will it help to tell you I'm not the guy I used to be? That the last thing I want to do is hurt her again?"

"It would help more if you told me why I should believe you."

"Because it's true. Whether it's because of the hit to my head or something else, I don't like the guy you and Marley and my father describe me as being back then. I don't like what I did to Marley, and I know I'm not the same person now that I was."

Angel pondered that a long moment, her gaze searching his face. He hoped she found whatever it was she looked for. If he got Angel to warm up to him, then maybe she would help him approach Marley and—

A Jeep roared to a squealing stop near where they sat. Marley's brother jumped out, his expression furious.

Angel rolled her eyes. "Here we go again."

Despite her words, however, Beau saw excitement flicker across her features before she banked the emotion for one of indifferent boredom.

He tried to set her foot aside to stand, but Angel was having none of it. Smiling deviously, she scooted closer to him on the bench and put her arms around him, easing her injured leg farther over his knee to hold him in his seat. "You better not be lying to me." She smiled up at him, murmuring the words between her gritted teeth. "Now, play along."

"Angel, what the—"

"Hello, Clay. Beautiful day, isn't it?"

Marley's brother stopped in front of them, his hands fisted, his breathing rough. He glowered at both of them. "What are you doing with *him?*"

Angel patted his chest, smiling innocently. "What does it look like?"

Beau glanced at Angel, wondering if she was deliberately trying to get him killed.

"I took a tumble while I jogged and Beau helped me. Isn't he sweet?"

"Sweet? The guy's a ba—"

"In fact, he just offered to take me back to his place to ice down my ankle."

Clay stepped closer. "You're not going anywhere with him."

Angel loosened her octopus hold and frowned up at Clay. "I suppose you think I ought to go with you?"

"Yeah, I do." To prove his point, Clay bent and scooped Angel up into his arms.

She sighed dramatically. "I suppose the devil I know is better than the one I don't. See you around, Beau."

Taking his chance to escape, Beau left them to it, turning back in time to see Angel wink at him over Clay's shoulder, twine her arms around the guy's neck and murmur something into his ear that had Clay stumbling over his own feet.

Beau chuckled at the sight. The guy didn't stand a chance, and he figured Clay deserved whatever Angel dished out.

Just as he did with Marley?

Suddenly he wasn't smiling anymore.

MARLEY HEARD A VEHICLE approaching and turned to see Beau arriving bright and early in a newer model Dodge. She'd seen the truck parked at the house the day she'd dropped Beau off and it must've been the one he'd driven the night he'd come to see her.

She ignored the shiver caused by Beau's stare and continued working. She hadn't spoken to him since her father's visit to the site, but that didn't mean she wasn't aware of his every movement in the time since. Still, he'd left her alone and for that she was grateful.

An hour later, he stood beside her. "Marley?"

She didn't respond. Maybe it was rude, but what else could she do? She'd spent every evening of the past week on the computer, researching her mother's medications and their side effects. And with every click of the mouse, fear settled deeper into the pit of her stomach.

"Look, just take it easy today, okay? I know you're trying to finish up, but you're pushing too hard. It's okay to take a break every now and again." He bent and left a bottle of water beside her.

Marley hesitated briefly, wanting to open her mouth, to at least mutter a thank-you for the kindness, but her guilt kept her quiet. It was best this way. For everyone. *Especially her mother.*

A sharp whistle ripped the air from somewhere across the street. Marley looked up to see Angel pulling into the driveway in her bright red sports car. Other than a quick glance to make sure the whistle hadn't come from Beau—and, no, she wasn't about to let herself overthink *that* too much—she ignored the men across the street and shook her head in bemusement when Angel got out and made her way toward her, all long legs and short shorts.

"What are you doing here?"

"I thought I'd come by and pay for my room and board today. Got an extra pair of gloves?"

Marley couldn't stop the laugh that escaped her lips. Angel had filled her cabinets with food, cooked most of the meals and cleaned the apartment from top to bottom. She'd paid for her room and board and then some. "Angel, you do not have to do this."

"I know." She shrugged. "I stopped by the shop, but Amy had her hands full with Eli. He kept dropping things every time I walked by. She mentioned you might need some help here." She wriggled her fingers. "Gloves?"

"In the truck." She grabbed the water bottle and followed Angel to the cab, opening the lid and rolling her eyes when more catcalls sounded as Angel bent over the seat. She could only imagine how Eli had felt given that the Buchanan crew couldn't keep their mouths shut. An extra pair of hands might help her out, but she had a feeling Barry and Beau's men wouldn't get anything done today. "Where were you last night? You didn't get in until late."

"Oh, sorry. I should've called."

"You don't have to report to me. I was just curious because we left at the same time yesterday and you were dressed for a run. Something happen?"

"Ah-ha! Here they are." Angel turned, triumphant. She yanked the three-dollar gloves over her fifty-dollar manicure. "Oh, you know how it goes. I ran into someone and got sidetracked."

There was no misreading her friend's expression. "Is that what they're calling it these days?"

"You know how those horses can be."

Marley choked on the water, laughing and coughing at the same time. This was why her parents had never wanted Angel hanging around. Angelique had always been adventurous. She wasn't easy by a long shot and never had been, but—

Was she really going to be like her parents and give Angel lectures after what she'd been through with her marriage? "Just be careful, okay? It's easy to get hurt on the rebound."

"That's why I'm here. So what are we doing today?"

Why she was there? Marley blinked up at her, envious of the extra inches in height. "Are you *sure* you want to do this?"

"Positive."

"All right, that's it. What's going on?"

"Nothing." A curious smile flickered over Angel's carefully glossed lips.

Marley frowned, eyeing her more closely. Angel had left for a run yesterday wearing very little makeup. Yet today she'd come to work outside in the dirt in full makeup?

"Come on, lighten up. I just thought I needed to get out of the apartment. Can't hide out forever, you know? So, I figured I'd give you a hand and—" she tilted her head toward the house across the street, a twinkle in her eyes "—those guys over there something else to talk about. Oh, who's the hunky-hunk with the goatee?" She shivered delicately. "You know, I never liked those before but *oh, baby.*"

Uh-huh. Something wasn't right and Marley's suspicions were starting to gel. "Did you have a run-in with Clay last night?"

Angel smiled and slapped her gloved hands together. "As a matter of fact, I did. Does he really think an apology is going to fix things? Your brother doesn't know who he's messing with."

Neither did Beau. She had five years of anger and resentment stored up. One kiss and some pretty apologies weren't going to fix those, either. "And that's why you're here? You're avoiding him?"

"Sort of."

"But?"

"Let's just say your brother's a bit too…tied up this morning to mess with anything."

Marley's mouth fell open. "Angel—you *didn't.*"

"If I don't come back after lunch—" she grinned "—don't come find me."

A laugh escaped before she could stop it. Talk about a comeuppance. No, Clay absolutely didn't know who he was messing with—otherwise he'd know Angel was no angel. "Have I told you how glad I am that you're back?"

"Does that mean you wouldn't mind if I stick around indefinitely?"

"Are you kidding me? I'd love it if you moved back. When will you decide?"

"Yesterday." She grinned. "I've made quite a few calls while I've been here. And you are now looking at the new owner of WLVV. Thanks to you, Delilah Kane is making a comeback."

Marley laughed, happy to have her friend back in town on a permanent basis. "Does Clay know?"

"No. And don't tell him. Your brother has a bit more groveling to do before I let him in on this particular secret."

CHAPTER FOURTEEN

BEAU STARED AT Marley and smiled when he saw her laugh at whatever Angel was saying. The sound floated on the breeze across the street to where he stood, and while he'd thought her pretty before, now—she was beautiful.

The wind whipped up and blew the first of the falling leaves through the air. Both women raised their hands to keep their hair out of their eyes and he found himself focusing on Angel as a memory stirred, flashing quickly in his mind.

A blond girl, blue eyes. Young, in her teens. She sat on the floor, legs drawn up, arms flailing as she tried to get the dark-haired guy tickling her to stop. She laughed like Marley, in full, breathless bursts of sound, belly laughs that—

"You okay, son?"

The image disappeared in an instant, leaving pain in its wake. He squeezed his eyes shut and rubbed his head. Pop had been doing that lately, checking on him if he thought he was remembering something, as if he was anxious for it to happen. Problem was it interrupted the memory, causing it to disappear before he could make any progress. "Yeah."

"You remember something?"

"Just someone laughing."

"Any names this time?"

"No."

His father hesitated, then indicated the kitchen at the back of the house. "Why don't you work on the lights in there? You'll be by the door that way."

He sighed, nodding. Pop had picked the room farthest away from the window where he stood watching Marley. Coincidence?

He didn't think so.

"SO HOW ARE YOU, BEAU? Any new memories this week?"

Beau settled himself on the comfortable leather couch for his regularly scheduled Thursday-afternoon appointment and grimaced tiredly at the shrink. Exhausted didn't begin to describe how he felt, but it was a good tired. Working hard made him feel better. "I remembered a blond girl with blue eyes." He'd learned after the first session or two that it was best just to open up and tell everything, then let Dr. Steinman go off on a tangent with his questions. The inquiries never brought up any new memories, but he'd admit to feeling less stressed about not remembering when he left the sessions. "She was laughing because someone tickled her."

"This Joe person?"

He shrugged, knowing Dr. Steinman meant well but not liking the process all the same. "I don't know. I can't see his face."

"Anything else?"

"Cut to the chase, Doc." He scooted down into the cushioned depths, getting comfortable. "What's it going to be this week? Fire away."

The doctor narrowed his gaze, then opened the notebook he carried into every consultation. After scanning his notes, he sighed and took off his glasses. "Tell me about Beau. Do you have friends?"

THANK GOODNESS for Friday, Marley thought as she tossed the last shovelful of mulch and moved along. She put a base of the less attractive stuff on the bottom before she went over it a second time with the "pretty" mulch. The first frost had covered the ground this morning, and the pressure was on to complete the second house before the Christmas rush hit and the weather turned cold.

January and February were the only months she considered slow. Normally she took classes and seminars and made sure the equipment was in good repair. October had flown by and Halloween had helped dwindle her fall merchandise down to a few remaining scarecrows and a handful of mums. Thanksgiving was around the corner with the start of the Winter Festival beginning Black Friday. Her To Do List overflowed, but she was thankful to be busy. It kept her from thinking too much about what was ahead of her.

Right now she focused on making sure her business was ready for Christmas. A landscaping business wasn't typically thought of as Santa's Toy Land, but since offering gift certificates and turning her garden center into a shopping haven of unusual accessories last year, things had picked up. People came to her to find items that weren't the chain store norm.

Her orders were arriving daily, and between meetings with WLVV's staff, dates with Clay and her night shift on-air, Angel had pitched in to help. She had a knack for decorating and displaying the merchandise to its best advantage. Angel had even decorated the Christmas trees Eli and Amy had helped her erect in the middle of the garden center, but hadn't had a chance to finish. While she started on the second house, she could complete the loose ends on her other projects.

Thanks to Beau.

Marley inhaled and sighed. Despite treating him like the plague, Beau seemed determined to help her out in an effort to make amends. Every time she turned around, she discovered a new surprise. Over the past couple weeks he'd unloaded her wheelbarrow and tools from the truck, as well as the bigger trees. And just this morning after she'd arrived, she'd gone into a Porta Potti and when she'd come out, Beau was unloading the last of the bagged mulch where she'd laid out her tools to work. But before she could take him to task for it, he'd dipped his head in a nod, rubbed the do-rag over his forehead to wipe the sweat from his brow and went back across the street, all without a single word.

She'd thought about it constantly. Hating him for not leaving town as she'd requested, and aching that he'd be so nice. She was limited by finances when it came to hiring an extra pair of hands, and Angel's and Beau's kindness meant more than either of them could possibly guess. If she didn't meet her deadlines the contract stated she could be replaced by another landscaper. She was the new kid on the block and this was her break; she didn't want to blow it. But why did he insist on helping her after everything she'd said to him?

Only one way to find out. Marley sighed again. She owed him her thanks if nothing else.

Taking the long way around the house to avoid the newly strawed lawn, she headed up the rough road to the next house. As she trudged along, her mind balked. What would her father say if he saw her?

Shaking her head and determining that she didn't care—her father hadn't spoken more than a few terse words to her since their argument—Marley bit her lip and made her presence known by stepping onto the plastic drop cloth layering the garage floor. An older man dressed in painter's whites added what looked to be the last coat on the far wall, while another man installed light fixtures on the ceiling.

"You looking for Mr. Buchanan?"

"Uh… Yes," she said, wondering which Buchanan the man would point her toward. What would she say if it were Beau's father?

"Around the side there."

She murmured her thanks and kept going. A foundation had been poured to begin work on a deck, and above that, wires hung out of their sockets on both sides of the French doors, the light fixtures on the ground nearby.

"Something wrong?"

Turning, she spotted Beau sitting propped against a nearby tree surrounded by fallen leaves. He didn't look good. "Are you sick?"

"Headache." A sad attempt at a smile lifted one corner of his mouth. "I get a migraine every time I remember something."

"Oh."

He closed his eyes with a grimacing nod. "What's wrong? One of the guys give you a hard time about something?"

"No. I—I came to say…thank you. For your help with the mulch."

"No problem."

"Eli's at the shop with Amy and I know I probably could delegate more to him, but with it being the last touch I wanted to make sure it was done right." She swallowed. "Anyway, thank you."

"You're welcome."

"Is there— Is there anything I can do for you? To return the favor? Get you some water?"

Beau's eyes were pain-filled slits. "Would you mind? It came on fast."

"No, I don't. I—I'll get some." She turned to go, but stopped when he said her name.

"The cooler's in the garage and there are pills in my lunch bucket beside it. It's red and has my name on it. Would you get them, too?"

"Sure. I'll be right back." Ignoring the curious looks she received when she returned to the garage, she found the pills and water and carried them back to Beau. She dropped to her knees beside him, reading the directions and shaking one of the tiny pills into her hand. "Here." He took the medicine without comment. "I'll leave the water for you and—"

"Don't go." Beau lifted his hand and brushed his knuckles against her knee lazily.

Shredded denim separated their skin, but his touch ripped through her like a lightning strike. She swallowed, too aware of the sensation. Of all the men in the world, why did it have to be Beau?

"Stay for a minute. Talk to me."

"Shouldn't you be quiet and sleep? Would my sunglasses help?"

"I can't sleep with sledgehammers banging on my brain." He grimaced. "But if you don't mind losing the glasses for a while, I'll take them."

"N-no, not at all." She leaned over him, slipping the plastic frames atop his ears. "Better?"

"Yeah. Thanks."

Biting her lip, she made herself comfortable beside him, the leaves crackling beneath her weight, the ones remaining on the tree rustling in the breeze. "What do you, um, want to talk about?"

"Anything." He smiled. "What's Angel been up to? She on the air today?"

Marley ignored the spike of jealousy she felt that Beau would ask about Angel, but then called herself an idiot. Everyone in town was talking about whether or not Delilah Kane would set the airwaves on fire with her sexy night show. And she couldn't help but wonder what her parents thought of Clay's relationship with her. *Whatever keeps their attention off you.*

"She's with Clay today. They're coming to terms with some things."

"He doesn't stand a chance, does he?"

A laugh caught in her throat. "Not much of one, no. She's had a thing for him for as long as I can remember. It's one of those love-hate things, though."

Beau shifted on the ground uncomfortably, his brows pulled low as he rubbed his head. "People change. Maybe they couldn't work it out before, but they can now."

Was he talking about Clay and Angel—or the two of them? "Why don't you lie down? You'd be more comfortable."

Beau rolled sideways, toward her, stretching out on the leaves. He pillowed his head on his arm with a sigh. Looking down at him, Marley liked being able to observe him unaware. Liked seeing him up close and vulnerable. It was often said that things came full circle but…how many times had she wished Beau would come back to her, begging for her? Hurting the way she'd hurt? Now as she took in the red scar on his forehead, she wished him no pain. She searched for it, but despite her earlier beliefs to the contrary, the anger that had been there five long years was gone.

"You said the headache was because you remembered something. What was it?" Unbidden, she brushed her fingertips over his forehead, removing a bit of leaf from his skin. She hesitated, then slid her fingers to his temple and rubbed gently, hearing Beau's deep sigh of relief and liking that she could help. All the while telling herself she'd do the same to anyone in such pain. That it was Beau meant nothing.

"A blond woman."

Her jealousy returned. Marley shook her head. She was *not* jealous. To be jealous in regard to a man like Beau would leave a woman perpetually upset. And indicate feelings for him that didn't exist. "Oh?"

"It's bothered me for a while. I kept picturing some guy tickling her, but I couldn't remember anything else. It was the same scene, over and over again."

"But you remembered more this time?"

"Yeah. It was Joe." A rough sound left him. "I don't know who he is, but his name is Joe and it was definitely him." He shifted as though agitated. "I asked Pop, but if he recognizes the name, he won't tell me. The shrink keeps hinting around that I lost a buddy overseas in the explosion that caused this, but he won't tell me who. He says when the time is right I'll remember. He wants me to schedule more sessions, but I've already had to reschedule a couple to help Pop get things done here."

And help her.

Beau opened his eyes and stared up at her, squinting behind the sunglasses, his knuckles rubbing over her knee once more but in a distracted manner. "Everything is happening too slow."

"It'll come."

"One of these days I'm going to remember us, Marley." It wasn't a comment but a promise.

"I know."

He frowned. "Saying I'm sorry doesn't change it,

but…I'd give anything not to have hurt you or your family."

She saw the truth written in every line of his face, in his eyes, the set of his mouth, the way his body was tensed and waiting for her response. His words weren't part of a game. If only her father and Clay could see his expression, maybe they could lose their anger. "I know. I'm sorry, too."

"You have nothing to be sorry for." He blinked drowsily. "I know it's too late for me to make things up with your family, but that talk we had about clean slates? Marley…it's almost Christmas and I'd really like to have that. Can we start over?"

Forgiveness. It seemed like everyone in the world wanted forgiveness for something. Clay and Angel. She wanted it from her parents. So much could be saved if people just let go of the pain they carried over things that didn't really matter.

But still she didn't answer. Couldn't. Not when she had such an explosive situation to handle with her parents. She'd avoided facing them and used work as her excuses, but she couldn't put it off any longer. Every day that passed allowed her mother to get worse. To fall deeper under the medications' spell. She had to do something. Take a stand even though the last thing she wanted was to hurt them again.

While she waged an inner battle of what to say and how, Beau's breathing turned heavy. His body relaxed in slow degrees and eventually his features began to smooth as the headache eased. Marley sat there a long time, watching over him, remembering things best left in the past. When it came down to it, she knew after his words and actions, she could easily let the past go and move on if the others would do the same. But they wouldn't, she knew it, and because of that she had to keep Beau at a distance.

Marley remained at his side a few more moments, enjoying the peacefulness until she forced herself to get up and walk back across the street to clean up her tools. She'd chosen Beau over her family once, she wouldn't do it again.

Minutes later, Barry Buchanan returned in the big red work truck and she paused, watching as he spotted Beau beneath the tree and went to check on him after speaking with one of his men. As though feeling her scrutiny, the older man turned and stared at her.

"Not good," she murmured under her breath, pinning a smile to her lips when he headed her way. "Hello, Mr. Buchanan."

"Miss Pierce. The men told me what you did. Thank you for getting Beau his medicine."

"It wasn't a problem, he's different now than he used to be." She said it as if it was to excuse what she'd done and clamped her lips shut, unable to believe she'd just blurted that out.

Beau's father stared at her a long moment, his expression troubled. "That he is." He shoved his hands into his pockets, his gaze flicking over the finished landscaping as though he were uncomfortable. *And you wonder why?* "Did you need to speak to me about something else?"

"There's no good way of saying this."

"I've discovered quick is usually better."

"Then here it is— I'd appreciate it if you stayed away from Beau. The headaches are worse when you're around."

She stiffened. Asking her to stay away was one thing, but to blame her for the headaches? "He had the headache before I talked to him, Mr. Buchanan."

"Maybe, but—Ms. Pierce, he told me about the baby." The man's head lowered, his gaze studying the ground at their feet. "I'm sorry about what happened, how it happened. You have no idea how much. But the shrink says it's best if Beau receives the information from him in a monitored setting, and I can't trust that you have Beau's best interests in mind after what happened between you. Telling him about the baby like that could've done major damage to him, physically, as well as emotionally."

Mr. Buchanan's words were laced with worry. "I see."

"Then you'll keep your distance?"

"We work on the same job site. Beau typically comes to see me, not the other way around." Except for earlier when she'd gone to see him.

To say thanks, her mind added.

But was that all? What about the day after he and Clay had fought at her apartment?

She'd checked on him. *That's all.* Marley swallowed, unable to lie to herself. She was drawn to him. Always had been. But now it was worse than ever, and she knew why.

"I'll talk to him about that. But if you do your part and tell him to steer clear—"

"I have."

"You need to be firm about it."

Her eyes widened. "I'm not sending him mixed signals."

Liar. Marley rubbed her forehead to ease the stress. Maybe she was. But if she did, it was because she was confused herself. She wasn't sure what she wanted anymore. Her family was so anti-Beau that if she so much as mentioned him they went off on a rant. No way could she be thinking of resuming any sort of relationship with him, friendship included. That would be pure insanity.

"I—I didn't mean to imply that." Beau's father flushed a ruddy red. "Just that he'll stay away if you're firm about him keeping his distance."

Marley stared at Beau's father and thought of her own. What else could she do but what was best for everyone involved? "If he approaches me again, I'll—I'll make sure I'm clear." Beau's father obviously saw her as a problem. The teenage pregnancy, Beau's amnesia. His son needed time to heal, not some woman from his past causing a setback.

"Thank you. Have a good day."

Marley watched as Beau's father walked back across the street, her gaze darting between the father and son. Have a good day?

She snorted. Her father, Clay, now Beau and his father. Men were *so* overrated. Give her some dirt, plants and a shovel any day.

CHAPTER FIFTEEN

MARLEY SPENT the rest of Friday and all weekend setting up her display for the start of the Winter Festival. The winners wouldn't be announced until December 20, and despite the problems in her life, she focused on the positive. She knew plants. She'd worked on her design titled A Christmas To Remember since the end of the competition last year and *this was her year.*

The entry fee was worth all the fuss. A local advertising company sponsored the event along with their clients, and the grand prize was a Web-site design and a year's free maintenance, twelve months of specially designed ads in the *Sentinel* and a boatload of exposure by local television and newspapers she couldn't otherwise get or afford. Add to it the new contacts she made just by setting up the display, and she'd learned to look forward to the Festival because it was the perfect way to end the year and plan for spring.

Best of all, by working here she'd managed to avoid Beau at the construction site, her parents *and* Clay and Angel making goo-goo eyes at each other. Clay really was making strides toward being the man

Angel needed, and she hated feeling jealous of their happiness. Would she ever find that herself?

Her thoughts drifted to Beau. Due to sporadic rain Monday and Tuesday, she hadn't been back to the development. She'd spent those days unpacking the last of the Christmas-themed products, erecting a barrier in front of her office using Alpine trees lit with white lights, working on shorter, easy-fix jobs for her other clients, and generally keeping herself busy so she wouldn't think of Beau and his father's request.

The bell on the door jingled. Marley turned expecting Amy and her smile froze when she saw Beau's broad-shouldered frame stepping inside. Without a word, he moved deeper into the building with barely a discernible limp and more warmth in his beautiful blue eyes than her own family held for her these days. "What are you doing here?"

Her tone stopped his approach. "I...brought you these." He held up the sunglasses she'd loaned him. "And I thought I'd drop by to let you know the crews have moved on to the third house. The land's clear and ready to start planting. I know you're eager to get it finished." He indicated the sunny, cloud-spotted sky outside the door. "It shouldn't take more than a day for the soil to dry up."

She'd driven by the construction site late last night and the ground had been littered with trash left behind from the Sheetrock hangers. Had he picked it up?

You know he did.

Wet from the rain, it wouldn't have been easy. The gesture caused her heart to give an extrahard thump in her chest, but instead of making her feel good, pain overshadowed the joy. Pain so deep, so intimate, she knew she was on the verge of making another huge mistake if she didn't establish some distance and fast.

"Thank you, but..." Feeling herself weaken, Marley stepped behind a chest-high shelf and gripped the edge. "You have to stop this, Beau. You have to—to not do what you're doing."

"What am I doing?"

"I know you cleaned up. I was there, I saw the mess."

His face darkened. Blushing? *Beau?* "It's not a big deal."

"It is a big deal! And I want you to stop. Do you hear me? Leave me alone. You do your job and I'll do mine, okay? If we keep it that way, our paths won't cross."

Beau lifted his hand and rubbed his fingers over his bristly jaw, the smile he'd worn coming into the garden center long gone. His blue eyes, such beautiful blue eyes, stared into hers. "What happened?"

She swallowed. "I just think it's time we stop pretending that everything is fine."

"I thought since our talk under the tree that we'd moved on."

She bit her inner lip. "Beau—"

The bell jingled again and Marley nearly swallowed her tongue when her mother's friend, Roberta, entered. Of all the worst possible—

"Hello, dear! My, how this place has changed

since I was here last! Oh! Sorry, I thought you were alone."

"No problem, Mrs. Forbes. Did you need something?"

Unlike Marley who was trying her best to ignore Beau's presence, Roberta couldn't take her eyes off him. "I don't believe I know you. I'm Roberta Forbes." She held out her hand.

Beau's big palm swallowed hers. "I'm—"

"Part of the construction crew at the new South Ridge Estates," Marley interjected quickly, earning a frowning glance from Beau. "He stopped by to give me a message, but he has to go. Please," she murmured, her gaze meeting Beau's quickly before she looked away, "let the site manager know I'll be there tomorrow to get started on the second house."

Beau hesitated, the few seconds seeming like hours. "Right."

A scowl marred his face, his eyes revealing all the emotions Marley didn't want to acknowledge. Hurt, pain, disappointment. She felt them, too, but she was only doing what was best to keep from causing more hurt. Why couldn't he see that? Do the same?

He stared at her, his gaze a physical caress. The act too long and too intimate if the expression on Mrs. Forbes's face was anything to go by. How was she going to get out of this?

"Nice to meet you, Mrs. Forbes. Marley." Beau moved to the door, discreetly setting her sunglasses on a nearby shelf on the way out. The cheery, jingling bell grated on her last nerve.

"Oh, my. I haven't spoken with your mother since she canceled our lunch date, but he—"

"Did you need something?"

The woman didn't falter. Nearing seventy, she wore her nosy personality on her smiling face as visibly as her Christmas attire. "Now, don't be embarrassed, dear."

"Why w-would I be? He's just someone from the job site."

Roberta seemed genuinely disappointed by the news. "Oh."

A cloud of perfume preceded Mrs. Forbes as she moved to the end of the shelving unit where Marley stood. Dressed in a bright red jumper and green shirt with dangling, red-nosed reindeer earrings, her mother's friend could've easily passed for Mrs. Claus.

"You know, dear, it's not my place to speak to you about these things, but I diapered you when you were born and I've known you your whole life. I feel bad for not spending more time with Donna, but she's so distant and I wondered if she's that way with you, as well?"

Taken aback by the woman's bluntness, she hesitated. "S-sometimes, yes."

Mrs. Forbes made a *tsking* sound. "I thought as much. Such a waste. So much time gone and nothing to show for it. She's your mother, of course, but we were all surprised by your behavior and pregnancy."

"Mrs. Forbes—"

"But there's no reason you shouldn't be flirting with that young man now."

She faltered. "Excuse me?"

Roberta smiled gently. "You're young and beautiful, Marley, and we all have our moments. You made a mistake, yes, but that was a long time ago." Mrs. Forbes made the comment with a nod of her head as though Marley couldn't have already realized that fact. "But as much as I love your mother, and I do, she's such a dear friend of mine—"

"I know."

"Well, then you know it's with love that I say it's time for her to let go of the past. I've told her so, many times."

Marley had to look away from Roberta and blink rapidly to clear the haze of tears blurring her vision. All of these years she'd put the blame on Roberta and her cronies for making her mother feel uncomfortable and the reality was that it was her mother who— She couldn't take it in. "You have?"

"Yes, dear. Things happen, but we can't be held accountable for childhood mistakes forever. Like I've told her, you've more than made good with yourself. Why, you donate flowers to the church to give the mothers every Mother's Day, you work the auxiliary's weedy beds and don't charge them." Her expression changed, became equally all-knowing and maternal. "I'm so sorry your mother hasn't been able to handle things, but I'm telling you now, dear, you can't let her inability to cope with life's ups and downs keep *you* from living." Roberta pointed toward the door. "That young man was gorgeous."

"Mrs. Forbes!" Marley laughed, hoping the sound disguised the emotion the woman's words had unearthed. "He's…just one of the electrical crew. That's all."

"If that's so then why didn't he simply call you?"

Marley ducked her head, her cheeks heating. Why, indeed. Obviously Barry Buchanan didn't know where his son was. And wasn't she doing the same thing she'd often thought her mother guilty of doing? Attempting to live up to someone else's rules and standards?

But they were her family, not strangers.

"See?" She patted Marley's forearm. "You think about what I said. Life's too short not to live for yourself, dear. You want your mother to be happy, we all do, but there comes a point where a decision has to be made." Roberta's eyes sparkled. "And given that that young man is making trips to come see you, I'd say you need to make it *soon* before the other girls in town get a look at him. Otherwise they'll have him under *their* tree for Christmas."

She nodded dazedly. The holiday was just around the corner. The town's streetlights were decorated with wreaths and carols had started appearing on the radio between the year's hottest hits. But despite the woman's words, all she wanted for Christmas was for her mother to wake up to reality and for her family to be a family again. For them to find forgiveness in their hearts for everyone needing it.

Including Beau?

The answer was yes—but that wouldn't happen. She knew very well that no one ever got everything they asked for.

BARRY WATCHED as Jack dropped the hammer he was using to nail in an electrical outlet box. The boy muttered a curse and picked it up again. "Something wrong?"

"No. Yes," he countered quickly. "Why was I such a jerk growing up?"

Dean snickered from another room, the open two-by-four studs allowing him to hear. "Got you tied up in knots, doesn't she?"

"Dean." Barry jerked his head toward the door. "Why don't you go get another roll of wire?"

The man shuffled off with a smirk on his face.

"What happened?" Barry asked once he was gone. He had to be careful these days and not slip up when he called the boy by name. Now that he knew the truth, the differences in the two men were obvious, making it that much harder not to distinguish them by name.

"I stopped by Marley's Treehouse on the way back from getting the supplies."

"Beau, I asked you to leave that girl alone."

He tossed the hammer aside and turned to sit on the floor. "I know. I wish I had now."

"Something happen?" Maybe the girl had kept her word and set the boy straight.

"I guess I just don't get how I could be so different. Then and now, you know?"

Barry opened his mouth to tell him the truth. Maybe it was time. Jack was stronger now, better able to cope. But then he thought of the consequences if the news was too much for Jack to handle, and closed his mouth again. *Soon.* Jack was just upset, but he'd settle down. "Things will work out. You're remembering more and more. Get yourself in shape and then you can decide what to do about the landscaper."

Keeping them apart was the only decent thing to do until the truth came out. He didn't want Jack or that girl doing something they regretted later. And while he never thought he'd be thankful for it, the damage Beau had done to the girl and her family worked to help him do just that.

Dean tossed the roll of wire into the house with a thud, ending the conversation. Jack got back to work nailing in the boxes.

Barry watched him, guilt tasting bitter on his tongue. Beau had been his flesh and blood, but Barry hadn't been blind to Beau's shortcomings as a son and as a man. He didn't like keeping the truth from Jack, but that guilt was nothing compared to the sadness he felt for liking the man Jack was proving to be more than he'd liked his own son.

Apparently, he wasn't so different from Jack's father after all.

BY THE END OF THE WEEK Marley had made some major headway at the second house but she'd yet to decide how to confront her mother about the pills. Time was speeding by and all her spare time was spent either at the garden center or at her display near the courthouse.

If she hadn't seen the box of pills with her own eyes, she probably would've laughed at anyone who suggested her mother—*her mother*—was living such an existence. An older, upper-middle-class woman wasn't exactly the image a person had when they thought of a drug addict.

She paused to stretch her back, her thoughts matching the layered, purple sky overhead. Eli had already mounded the soil and because of the design, only the front of the house was to be planted along with a small island in the yard. Perennials had already died back, but come spring they'd flourish.

Low-growing shrubs interspersed with day lilies lined the walk to the porch, and in an open area between the entry and the wall of the garage, she'd added a medium-sized white trellis and a red climbing rose. She'd planted a two-year-old Bradford pear in the island out front, and added a stone bench and what would eventually be a colorful assortment of black-eyed Susans, more bright orange-and-yellow day lilies and three Knock Out roses that were virtually maintenance free but smelled heavenly. Winding through the center, she made a miniature river of rock with small round stones that would give the island texture and added a path to the bench.

Marley found a bare spot and crouched, spreading more mulch. With a thick layer of insulation against the winter ahead, none of the plants should be lost. This part of northern Kentucky didn't get a lot of snow, and the plants had plenty of time to acclimate before the ground froze.

A thump sounded and echoed off the house. Marley startled, glancing up to locate the source.

"Let's go, son. It's been a long week."

Barry Buchanan climbed into the diesel truck but left the driver's door open, one leg hanging out of the cab.

Beau emerged from the newly roofed house and shut the door behind him. "You go on, I'll be right there."

Barry Buchanan murmured something she couldn't make out, but she saw Beau nod in response. The truck's brake lights blinded her when they flashed on, and she squeezed her eyes shut. Seconds later the truck was gone.

Beau turned and, hesitating, lifted a hand in her direction. She smiled before she caught herself and ducked her head, hoping that the dim light of dusk covered her mistake.

She glanced at her watch and decided to call it a day, as well. Seeding the grass and spreading the straw would have to wait until Monday, but it was a good job for Eli.

Marley gathered up the plastic flowerpots, the weed blocker and mulch bags she'd tossed aside, fatigue dragging at her every step. When she couldn't fight the need to keep Beau at arm's length, she knew it was time to go home. Despite Roberta's urging to flirt, things had to be settled with her mother before she could ever even remotely consider…

What? Consider what? Did she *have* any options where Beau was concerned?

"Hey."

She stilled. How had she missed noticing him coming over?

He bent and grabbed a rake. "Let me help you."

"I can do it. You go on home. It's been a long week and you're—you're still recovering."

"It's been nearly three months. Other than the memory thing, I'm fine." He picked up the bucket she'd used to water everything next. "I saw your display for the Winter Festival. It looks great."

"Thanks. But no one puts out more than their basic design at first. The best parts are the finishing touches that go out the night of the judging. I put a lot of thought into the setup, though."

"It shows. Where'd you find the wagon?"

"One of my customers. Her husband makes them." Silence. "Look, Beau—"

"I'm not leaving you here alone so don't ask. You don't want me hanging around in your personal life. I get that. But I heard today that some equipment was stolen and things were messed with. I'll leave when you do."

"It was probably just some kids playing around. Stupid stuff like—" She bit her lip at yet another blunder.

"Like I used to do?" He acknowledged that with a slow nod. "Maybe so, but there were signs of a party in the woods, and that kind of playing could mean trouble. I'll help you pack up and then we'll both call it a night."

The sun had set behind the hill well over an hour ago and dusk was quickly turning to night. The temperature was dropping, and before long it would be pitch-dark. She'd admit to not wanting to be there alone. The development resembled a ghost town when empty, and in the last hour alone she'd jumped a good half-dozen times because of the eerie sounds she heard in the woods. Animals scurrying in the treetops, things falling. She was jumpy because of nuts?

She was jumpier because of Beau.

Some truths had to be faced. “Fine,” she murmured, relenting. “Let’s get me packed up then.”

Ten minutes later she wiped her hands on her pants. The air was crisp and fresh and she could see her breath, but she’d layered on clothes and was comfortable. “That’s it for me. Thanks.”

“You’re welcome. I’ll follow you home. Make sure you get there okay.”

“It’s out of your way.”

“I don’t mind. It’s a good night for a drive. I’ve done it a lot lately.”

“Where do you go?”

“Down to the dam. I stare at the river and…” He shrugged. “Come on, let’s go.”

Without comment, Marley climbed into her truck. The whole way down the nearly deserted road she listened to promotion spots for Angel’s program, and thought of Beau sitting in his truck and staring at the water. Then she looked behind her and liked that he was there, following her. The sight brought comfort whether she wanted it to or not.

The ID tags Beau wore around his neck had caught her attention more than once the last few times they’d talked. They’d become a symbol of change to her, and represented his growth as a person. Too bad her parents and Clay would never recognize it, much less believe it.

Marley turned into the alley behind her apartment and slowed. Would he follow her?

Did she want him to?

Shaking her head at herself, she decided she did. Just to talk. She liked that they'd actually had several conversations now that hadn't disintegrated into fights, and even though she knew she was playing with fire, she couldn't seem to help herself.

Beau pulled into the alley and slowed. She parked the truck in the area she used as an equipment garage and locked up. Still, he waited. Her heart picked up speed. *Don't make me decide.* Because she already knew what her decision would be and it wasn't one Clay or her parents would approve of. She was tired of living for everyone but herself and never gaining their approval regardless.

Without a word, Beau got out and took the empty water cooler from her hand. He followed her into the building and up the enclosed stairs to her apartment. Outside her door, she paused.

Ever since she'd noticed the changes in him, she'd been drawn to him. Stupid of her, but true. Why couldn't she like some nice, normal guy?

"Beau, I'm sorry I've been acting so strange lately. Being nice and then telling you to go away. I know it's probably been confusing, but if my presence causes you more pain a-and headaches, I thought it was best. I've been so concerned about you being here in town with my mom and family, and trying to avoid another fallout with them that… I'm trying to say that you're right. After our talk, things were different, better, but I don't want to cause either one of us more pain."

He frowned at her words. "Marley, you don't make the headaches worse. Why would you think that?"

"Your father said— I guess it was just his way of saying I add to the stress you're under to remember."

Beau's hair had grown over the last two months, and Marley curled her fingers into her palms to keep from reaching out to touch it, to smooth the wind-mussed length brushing his ear into place.

"The headaches come and go as they please, you have nothing to do with them."

"Good." Relief flooded her. "I'm glad." She fiddled with her keys, unlocked her door and opened it slightly. "I—I guess I'd better go in and let you go take that drive. Thanks for seeing me home."

"Marley— Wait." He dropped the cooler to the carpeted floor and took her arms in his hands. "I remembered something today. Something that didn't make sense. I saw a casket…a funeral with a tiny casket at the front of a church. You said I wasn't around when our baby died, but what about when the baby was buried?"

"You still weren't around." She swallowed tightly, the memories of her daughter's death overwhelming her for a brief moment.

"It was white with pink flowers on it. A big bouquet of pink flowers—roses. It was in a church and there were *a lot* of people."

"You weren't there." She sucked in a deep breath. "And that's not what the f-funeral was like. We—we didn't have it in a church because my parents felt— It was at the funeral home. And it was private. M-me and Clay and my p-parents. And Angel," she added softly. "That's all."

He stared at her, one hand lifting to his forehead where he rubbed hard. "But I *felt* it. I felt her passing. I felt the pain of losing her. If it wasn't the baby we had—"

"You weren't there, Beau. You—You must be thinking of a—a different baby. A different funeral. I'm sorry." Beau's hands latched on to her arms and he gripped them, as though he held on to keep himself standing, his eyes closed.

"I hate this," he growled, his voice revealing the depth of his frustration, his gaze holding hers. "I hate what I did to you. I hate that I…that I wasn't there to see my baby buried." Beau dropped his hands and paced across the short landing. Away from her, back again. "I *hate* who you say I was. And I hate myself for not being man enough— What will it take to convince you that I'm not him anymore, Marley? I don't know why I ever acted like that, but I'm *not* him."

The dim overhead light allowed her to make out his features. She stepped in front of him so that he stopped, lifted her hands and placed them on his chest, barely daring to breathe. He'd changed on a deeper level. She recognized it in her marrow, knew it in her soul. And more than anything, she liked the man he'd become way more than she should. Too much, given the circumstances. So many things were wrong. Messed up wrong.

Except for this.

Despite her railing at him—justifiably or not—he hadn't once said a word against her. Hadn't tried to make her feel guilty or sleazy for their brief connection. Some guys would have. Angel's ex-husband was a good example of the type of man who would've tried to belittle her.

Beau had helped her, talked to her, apologized many times over. He'd shown her he wasn't the same man by carrying a stupid tree. So many little things, but they were important things. Gestures that described the man inside him better than any smooth lines or prettily worded apologies could.

The list grew in her head, one by one, and still, Beau stood, silent and tall, his expression revealing and vulnerable in a way that tore past the last of her defenses and opened the very gates to her heart that he'd closed so long ago.

Her mind screamed a frantic *No, no, no!* but her heart refused to listen. This moment was about way more than the past, more than regrets. It was about believing in a person's soul, in their goodness. Believing in the man she saw standing before her.

Marley inhaled, hesitated, but deep inside she knew what she wanted, knew she couldn't go back. "I believe you."

CHAPTER SIXTEEN

SHE'D READ THAT three little words could change everything. Most people meant *I love you,* but her *I believe you* had the same effect.

Beau's expression tightened, his nostrils flared and his mouth parted to draw in a rush of air. A rough sound left his throat and an instant later he lowered his head, his mouth claiming hers with such seductive force and raw sensuality that she forgot to breathe. Forgot that she should be frightened because she'd walked this path before.

All she could do was feel. Want. *Need.* She twined her arms around Beau's neck and held on, knowing this man was everything the boy she'd known wasn't. One kiss turned into two, and she was vaguely aware of Beau's hands sliding low and lifting her up until she was pressed breast to thigh along his hard frame. They groaned at the contact, at the erotically painful pressure.

"Beau…inside."

He held her safe in his arms while he pushed the door open, turned and shut it by pressing her to its varnished frame. Over and over his head dipped so he could kiss her, as if he couldn't help himself, then he'd break the contact and journey somewhere else to kiss and nip and lick. Back again.

They tore at each other's clothes, pulled off layers of shirts, shoved the material aside as quickly as possible. She was desperate to feel his skin, his strength, unable to believe the fumbling, okay experiences of their past could ever be replaced by this frantic desire to know him again. To believe the sad, hesitant voice in her head whispering that if her parents and Clay weren't in the picture, then maybe she and Beau might have a chance because this—this was special. Passion as it was meant to be.

"Hold on to me." Beau buried his nose into her neck and groaned, his hands shoving her panties down. "I want you so much." He kissed his way up to her mouth, dipped his tongue inside. After a long, drugging kiss, he pulled back slowly, smiling seductively as his teeth latched on to her lower lip.

Gentle pain shot through her, straight to the center of her, and Marley closed her eyes with a moan. She tried to slow the galloping pace of her heart, but it didn't work. Five years ago had been all about curiosity and hormones, freedom, but this was more. Bad timing, but—*more.*

Tomorrow morning she'd deal with the regrets and the pain, mourn what might have been if her family weren't so important to her, but not now. Not now.

His hands tightened, pulled her closer against the cradle of his hips as he pressed her into the door. His fingers slid low, until she clung to him, her nails biting into his shoulders in an urgent bid to anchor herself and not feel so much.

Beau sucked on her nipple until she arched her body into his, longing to get closer, inside him the way she wanted him inside of her. The need built to an unbearable degree, one he didn't seem in any hurry to satisfy. *"Beau."*

He chuckled at her tone, groaned at the way she rolled her body against him like a wave, touching, surging. With a low murmur and a breath-catching stroke to make sure she was ready, he shifted, lifting her with an arm around her waist, lowering her and joining them with a silky-smooth glide. Tightness, need. Her head fell back against the door as Beau entered her, each nudge and push ending in a grind that maximized the experience and left her gasping. He took her mouth the same way he took her body, kissing her deeply, until she came in a breathy, teary cry of bone-melting satisfaction.

Three strokes later, Beau's hoarse groans filled her ear.

THE FIRST THOUGHT that entered Marley's head when her brain reconnected with her traitorous body was thank goodness she was on the pill. At the moment she couldn't think about the other potential dangers of not using a condom. Those recriminations and fears would come later. Unprotected sex was like playing Russian roulette—and with Beau's sexual history being what it was there would be five bullets instead of one.

"I can practically hear your mind churning." He smoothed the tense muscles of her back, drawing a sigh of pleasure from her before she could stop it. She shook her head to clear it and wound up nose-first in his neck. Despite a hard day's work, he smelled good.

You're so easy.

"We didn't use a condom." She felt his body tense, then relax. Not the response she'd expected.

"Would a baby be so bad?"

She blinked. That *definitely* wasn't the response she'd expected. Marley raised her head to stare up at him, acutely conscious of the fact her feet didn't touch the floor because he still held her pressed to the door with his body.

"I'm on the pill, so there's nothing to w-worry about, but yes— I mean, no, a baby isn't a *bad* thing, but…right now it's the last thing we need to be risking considering." She tried to distance herself, but he wouldn't let her.

Beau framed her face in his hands and smiled gently. "Things are going to be different this time."

This time?

He moved back slightly, just far enough that she could lower her legs to the floor. When her toes touched, the shock of the cold came with a truckload of fear. How could she want someone so much, knowing her family would never accept him?

Fantasizing about the man she'd come to describe as the new and improved Beau was one thing, but she didn't do this lightly. She hadn't been with anyone since the last time she and Beau had been together. At eighteen, it had been a mistake. Now it was an example of her actively breaking her own heart.

"Marley, you're freaking me out here. Are you okay?"

Inhaling shakily, she nodded. Things *were* different this time. She knew what she wanted out of life. What she needed. Tonight would only last so long and in the morning everything would look a whole lot different. "I need a shower."

Beau hesitated, his gaze searching. When she didn't say anything else, when she didn't hand him his clothes and say, *Thanks, for the big-O,* he smiled. "That an invitation to join you?"

The husky timbre of his voice sent shivers through her and she told herself she deserved tonight. One night of happiness and comfort. One night to make up for the past. "If you'd like to."

"I'd like to." He pressed a kiss to her forehead, her cheek. "Marley, this isn't the time but—I'd like to try to talk to your brother, your parents. See if we can work things out."

She shook her head firmly back and forth. Beau was the one being gullible now. "I don't want to talk about them. I want a shower and food a-and…you."

He stroked his knuckles down her cheek, the touch soothing and arousing at the same time. "Where's the shower?"

Inanely self-conscious, she took his hand in hers and led him through the darkened apartment to the bathroom. There she flipped on the single overhead light and avoided his gaze. She was absurdly nervous given what they'd just done, her body flushed fluorescent pink. Not a good color for a redhead.

After turning on the taps, Marley bit her lip and stepped inside. Beau followed. He grabbed the soap first, smiling his sexy, bad-boy grin before lathering up his hands and smoothing them over her shoulders and her arms to her breasts. Washing her gave him great pleasure if his rough breathing was anything to go by. Beau turned her this way and that, letting the shower's massaging head rinse the soap away before he grabbed her shampoo bottle. "Turn around."

She did as ordered, sighing when his hands rubbed the shampoo into her hair, enjoying the experience for what it was without putting too much thought into the fact it would never happen again. Beau pulled her against him so that her breasts pressed against his chest while he angled her head with his hands, careful not to let the suds run into her eyes.

"Beautiful."

Smiling at his silliness, afraid to name what she thought she saw in his eyes when he looked at her because the reality was that it was only the reflection from her own gaze, she reached for the soap and slid him a glance, noting the way his body tensed in preparation.

She rubbed the soap between her hands and set to work washing his shoulders and chest, gentling her touch over the red scar on his shoulder. Over his rock-hard abdomen. "Turn around," she ordered, smiling when his expression of anticipation turned into a frown at the request.

"I like the view this way."

"Too bad," she countered, unused to playing the teasing games couples play.

They weren't a couple.

She bit her lip, deciding it was best to stick with the moment and nothing else. "Turn around."

Beau followed directions. He lifted one muscled arm to brace against the shower wall and propped his forehead on his fist.

The broad plane of his back called to her and she spread her fingers wide, touching, smoothing over his shoulders and down, down, loving the soft feel of his skin over hard muscle. Loving—

"There's more interesting parts you know… Marley?"

She swallowed, frowned, her fingertips still even though she searched his back with her gaze. *Where was it?*

Beau had been injured the first time she'd met him, the scar fairly big—as wide as her hand and long. *Fresh.* Too large and deep, the skin too damaged by the burn, to have simply faded away.

So where was it? Wrong place? She pictured it in her mind, dropped her hands to where it should have been.

No. No. *It wasn't there.* No scar tissue, no scar. Nothing but perfectly smooth skin. Marley jerked away from him so fast she almost fell out of the shower.

"What the— What's wrong?"

Gasping, she got out of the shower as quickly as possible and grabbed a towel from the bar nearby. She held it in front of her like a shield.

It was him. *Beau.* Bigger, older and more appealing. But where was the scar? "Where is it?" Her voice was shaking, almost unrecognizable. She cleared her throat and tried again. "Where *is* it? The scar y-you had when we met?"

He stared at her, his brows pulled low over his eyes. "What scar? I'm covered in scars, you'll have to be more specific."

A near-hysterical laugh emerged from her throat before she could squelch it. "You had a scar on your back and h-hip when we met. About four inches wide a-and all across your back! It was from gasoline, a *burn.* I-it wouldn't have just faded away, where is it?"

The man standing before her looked at her as if she'd lost her mind, but no amount of time, especially not a few years, could've changed his appearance. Not like that.

He turned off the water with two flips of the knobs, looking around for something to dry off with. She grabbed a towel from a stack on the shelf and threw it at him.

He caught it with one hand. "Marley, calm down."

"You got it riding motocross. You were practicing and weren't wearing your full g-gear. You said you crashed and the bike came down on you. It burned you and…it was on your back," she repeated, desperate for him to smack his forehead and say, *Oh, yeah, that one,* but he didn't.

His eyes stared into hers with complete confusion, the color fading from his skin. "You're serious."

You think? She clamped a hand over her mouth, but a whimper escaped. High and shrill and borderline hysterical. "Dear God, what have I done?" She shook her head. "Who *are* you?"

"Marley—"

She ran for the bedroom, grabbing the robe at the foot of her bed and shrugging it on as she went, her hands shaking so badly she barely managed to tie the belt. She focused on the details, searching her memories for clues. Answers. *Oh, God.*

"You're not Beau."

"Marley, look at me. Of course, I'm—"

"*You're* not *Beau!*"

CHAPTER SEVENTEEN

HE STEPPED FORWARD, grasping her shoulders lightly. "That's ridiculous. Calm down and—"

She lunged to the side, desperate for distance, for the ability to think straight. Explanations. She needed a rational explanation. If he could give her that—

What had she done? What had she *done?*

Panicked, she held up her hands to ward him off. Surprisingly, he stopped. Marley backed to the door of the bedroom and flipped the light switch, taking in every minute detail of his appearance.

Sixteen days total. That's all she'd had with Beau and that was five years ago. She hadn't even seen him every one of those days. Could anyone remember specific details about a man who was basically a stranger?

"You're not Beau."

He swore, the sound full of anger and disgust. "Enough with that, Marley, I get it. You're having second thoughts, right? It was fun, but what I said about working things out with your family got to you, didn't it? Let's get dressed and we'll—"

"You're not *Beau.*"

"Of course, I am!"

"You're *not!*" Shaking her head she ran for the living room, throwing open a closet door and grabbing her only means of self-defense. An old golf putter of Clay's in hand, she turned just as B—

Her knees nearly buckled when she realized she didn't even know his name. "Get out!"

"What the— Put that down."

He looked pale. But of course he was. The only thing worse than someone actually *being* Beau Buchanan was someone trying to pretend he was Beau. She almost snickered at the thought. If it acted like a duck and looked like a duck…

Swearing, he grabbed the ID tags around his neck. "Look. Look! Right there. See?"

Marley didn't bother looking. She knew what she knew. She wasn't sure how it was possible, but she knew. Question was why would he do such a thing? In the book, Sommersby had wanted his stepbrother's plantation, his wife, his life, but she didn't have anything. A business barely in the black, but nothing else.

She'd slept with him thinking he was Beau, which was bad enough after the way Beau had treated her, but… *This was all a lie.* "Stay away from me." She raised the putter higher and kicked his discarded clothes toward him. "Get dressed and g-get out."

Shaking his head and glaring at her, he dropped the towel, grabbed his underwear and yanked it on, all the while maintaining eye contact with her. "Own up to it, Marley. You're having second thoughts, but there's no need to pull a stunt like this. I thought after everything we've been through that we had a chance. Why are you doing this to us?"

"There is no us! You're not even *you!*" She was rational enough to realize that last statement didn't make sense, but nothing made sense at the moment. She'd traded one jerk for another and fallen for lies again. *Again!*

The sexy smile, the crooked grin and the dimple that—

This Beau—this *person*—didn't have a dimple.

She choked on a sob. "Was this some sort of sick joke?"

"Sweetheart—"

"Who *are* you? Why would you *do* this to me?"

Footsteps sounded in the hall and a split second later the door to her apartment burst open. Angel took one look at his half-dressed state and her eyes went wide. "Oh, I should've known."

"He won't leave." The statement came out as a whimper.

Angel put herself between them. "You've got *two seconds.*" Her normally sexy, sultry voice was drawn and tight. "You said you wouldn't hurt her. How could you do this to her again? Clay's on his way here and if he doesn't kill you, I will."

Marley sucked in a sharp breath at the news. If her brother walked in on this— "Get out!"

He swore, pulled his pants up his long legs and tugged his shirt over his head. "I'm the one who got played in all of this, didn't I? I can't remember what happened so what better time to get even and treat me like I treated you, is that it?" He stared at her, his gaze boiling with anger.

"No."

A raw burst of frustration escaped his lips. "No? You think accusing me of— If I'm not Beau, who the hell am I?"

"I don't know—I don't care! Th-think whatever you like but don't you ever, *ever* come back."

He stood there, his jaw flexing with his anger, his hair messed from the shower and his hurry to dress. Then with a look of utter bitterness and pain and too many emotions to name, he walked out and took her heart with him. She was a fool. She was such a fool!

"Are you okay?"

"No." She wouldn't ever be okay again. The sound of the Hemi engine roared to life and faded away with a squeal of tires.

"Come sit down."

"I need to— Clay's coming. You need to go and—and tell him I'm sick. A cold or s-something."

"I'm not going anywhere."

"You *have* to. I can't— Why are you here?"

Angel helped her over to the couch and made her sit. "You've been working so hard and been so down lately, we wanted to take you out for some fun. Clay said he'd meet me here before I started my show tonight."

"You can't tell him about this."

"Marley—"

"You *can't*. Angel, what did I do? I knew better than to believe. To do this *again*. Why did I think he was different? Why didn't I see the changes before—" She pulled the sleeves of her robe down to cover her hands and buried her face in the folds. "If they find out what I did..."

"Shh. It'll be fine. It's okay. Just take a deep breath and start from the beginning. What happened?"

The scene replayed in her mind, and she turned into Angel's comforting embrace and told her the unbelievable tale. "Please, Angel," she finished. "Please, you have to promise me. You can't tell Clay about this."

"She can't tell me about what?"

HE DROVE PAST Marley's Winter Festival display on the way home. The lights were on, making it the quintessential Christmas scene. The design showcased her skills and imagination.

What an imagination it was.

It wasn't true. He couldn't consider the possibility because it *wasn't* true. If it was—

The look on Marley's face.

He held on to the wheel so tightly his knuckles cracked. Most of the houses he passed were lit as brightly as Marley's display, a blur of color as he raced by. If he wasn't Beau...

"She's lying." His head started to pound and he willed away the pain. Christmas was less than two weeks away. Pop had said he hadn't made it home last Christmas and even though it had probably meant frozen dinners or a meal at Chang's like they'd done for Thanksgiving, he'd been looking forward to it.

"*Dammit.* She was mistaken. Upset." Under a lot of stress with preparing for the competition and keeping her business afloat, the job site and most definitely her family. They hated him and she knew it. Marley regretted making love with him; that's why she'd freaked out.

But the look on her face.

He banged his hand against the steering wheel until his palm ached. It wasn't true. What kind of woman played games with a guy who couldn't remember?

The kind that wanted revenge.

That was the only answer. He'd hurt her and her family. Badly. So much so she didn't want to be seen with him. He thought back to the times he'd talked to her, how she'd step around to the side of the houses out of clear view and at her shop— She didn't even let him introduce himself to that lady. She'd sat beside him under the tree but that was only because he'd guilted her into it. They'd been virtually out of sight there, too.

God knows she had the power to bring him low. They might not have spent that much time together, but the time they had spent had been quality. Figuring things out, talking about the past. Moving on. She'd made him feel things he—

He shut those thoughts off. He'd liked Marley, could easily see why he'd hooked up with her years ago even though he didn't have a clue why he'd treated her the way he had. *But why accuse him of being someone else?*

The truck sprayed gravel as he skidded into the

drive. He pictured her tonight, head back, gasping as he made love to her.

God, don't let it be true.

Marley's face, her expression—this wasn't a game to her and his anger boiled over into rage. This wasn't revenge unless she was one hell of an actress. The horror in her eyes when she questioned him about the scar said it all.

It wasn't true. It would mean that Pop—

He barged inside the house, uncaring that the door crashed into the wall when he flung it open. His head felt as if someone was taking an ice pick to it, but nothing was going to stop him from getting the answers he needed.

"Pop?" What was it about the way Marley had looked while she screamed at him? "Pop!"

"How could you do *that to her?"*

He stumbled at the memory. A woman's voice. Not Marley's, not Angel's. Definitely not his mother's.

Chills racked him as pain ripped through his skull like a buzz saw. Marley's expression, the revulsion. The blond girl's face. *"Pop!"* He lifted his hand and rubbed, careening off walls and furniture to get to the hutch on the far side of the room, vaguely registering Pop's footsteps hurrying down the hall.

There were photos in the hutch. He'd looked at them for hours on end already, but maybe now… He had to prove Marley wrong. Pop wasn't lying.

"She's lying*! I didn't—Jack! Jack, get Pop! Go get Pop!"*

"Son? What's wrong? Beau?"

His head pulsed with every beat of his heart. He stood with his hands braced on the hutch, the image—Joe and…Jack. Joe had looked right at him when he'd said that. Screamed at him, called him…*Jack.*

"You've got a bad one. Come sit down. I'll get your pills."

He didn't move. If he let go of the hutch he'd fall flat on his face. "Where are they?"

"Where are what?"

"The pictures. Where are all the pictures?" Still holding on, he turned toward his father, squinting from the pain streaking through his head, the room moving in odd waves. He wasn't going to believe it until… "Mom liked to take pictures. She took a lot of them. Said she'd rather be behind a camera than in front of it." Another piece of the puzzle. Bits and snatches came at him faster and faster, unfurling from the black stream in his mind. *"Where are the pictures?"*

Pop's expression changed. Became…guarded? *No.*

"Son—"

"Where are my school pictures? The—The one of me in Little League? The one of me and, what was her name? Annie or Andrea or—Andie! We went to the sixth-grade dance together. She wore a blue dress and Mom took pictures of us."

Pop ran his hands over his balding head, his face taking on a reddish hue, his eyes bright. Tears? No. He wouldn't cry unless…

"Come sit down before you fall down. I'll call the doc—"

"I can't wait anymore!" He groaned at the pain his

own voice caused. "Marley said— Pop, where's the damn pictures?" The suffocating feeling was taking over again. The same sensation he'd had in the hospital when he'd been trying to wake up and couldn't. He wanted to wake up *right now* and realize it was all a bad dream. It had to be a bad dream because no one would let a person believe a lie like this.

"What did she say to you?"

He laughed, but the noise that came out of his chest was nowhere close to the right sound. "She said I'm not me—*Beau.*"

"Son—"

"She's lying." He raised a hand and grasped his ID tags, holding them tight and trying to ignore the expression on his father's face. No. *No*. "I'm Beau."

"No, son. No…you're not." His father—*Barry* said it gently, his voice low, a short, bare whisper. The man stepped closer, his eyes red and full of tears he made no attempt to hide. "I'm sorry. You have no idea how much. I regret… She's right. You're not Beau. Beau—my Beau—died back in September in the same bombing that injured you. You were friends, *good* friends, but you're not him."

He ripped the tags off with a jerk and slammed his hand into the glass door of the hutch. The glass broke, slicing into his knuckles, but he welcomed the pain. Anything was better than the dazed numbness overtaking him.

"Let me—"

"How? *Why?*" Glass crunched beneath his boots when he shifted his feet and pressed his forehead to the cool wood. The anger inside him too much. He had to stay calm enough to get the answers he demanded. Had to think. "*Why* didn't you tell me? *Why* did you lie and let me believe I was your son?"

"I didn't know at first. I swear, I didn't know. And then I couldn't bring myself to tell you. I didn't want to believe it, don't know how it could've possibly happened. I'm to blame for a big part of what you're feeling right now, Jack, but you and Beau looked so much alike." He wiped a shaking hand under his nose. "Do you remember that?"

Barry hesitated, then hurried away to grab a fresh towel from a drawer. Back again, he pressed it against the cuts on his hand.

There it was—*Jack*. The friend Dr. Steinman had told him about?

He lifted his too-heavy head and watched dazedly while Barry wrapped the material around his hand and tied it into a thick knot, the dog tags sticking to his palm. He didn't remember anyone named Beau or *Jack*.

"You could've been brothers. Back when you two met, we traced what we could of your history, but couldn't find any connection to explain the resemblance. In the hospital with the cuts and bruises and swelling—the bandages… I should've been able to tell, but they said you were Beau and I never once thought something like this could have happened. I was just so grateful my son was alive, I never thought he—*you*—weren't him. You were wearing Beau's tags—that's how they identified you afterward. I brought you home and—and the boy they sent home to your family— That was Beau."

"Are you sure?"

Barry closed his eyes at his bitter, sarcastic tone, nodded slowly. "There were other soldiers injured but you—*Beau* was the only fatality. You looked so much alike. I've no doubt it's him. And now that you know, we can get the answers you need, Jack. Figure out what happened and—and get Beau back to where he belongs."

The chain stuck out from beneath the towel, tinged with his blood. Beau's tags. He stared at them, wishing he felt something more than a freaked-out sense of nothing. "How long have you known? Why didn't you *tell me?*"

"I've known a few weeks now."

Weeks?

"We need Dr. Steinman here. Jack, son, I waited to tell you because I didn't want you traumatized when you found out. That girl—"

"Don't. Don't say a word against her. She told me the truth, you didn't."

Pop—*Barry* paused.

He glared at the man, stared into eyes so like his own. The rational part of him heard the words about the ID tags and mix-up, but there was a part of him that raged because he'd lived a lie, carried another man's sins. And for what? "You owe me the truth. When did you find out? How long were you going to let this go on?"

Air rasped through Barry's chest. "I noticed little things, but I didn't give them much thought. Beau had changed a lot over the years, so I passed those off as that. Calling me Pop when Beau had always called me Dad. The way you picked up around here when Beau—" He laughed softly. "Beau didn't lift a finger. H-He… Beau always liked to sleep on a pillow of a mattress, the softer the better. I saw you doing that stuff, but it didn't register. And then you brought home the fish. Beau and I—we're allergic."

"Allergic?" He remembered that night, how pale Barry had been, the way he'd collapsed. "I could've killed you."

Barry smiled a lopsided smile, looking old and worn-out. "It was the truth I hadn't wanted to see, there in unmistakable detail. The stress of that and fatigue. I'd gotten off track with my meds after starting the job and traveling overseas. It wasn't your fault, Jack." He raised his head, looking sad and broken. "Everything's going to be okay."

"How can you say that?"

"Because I've had time to cope with the news. Mourn. You haven't, but it'll come. Regardless of whose tags you hold, son, it doesn't change the outcome. The bomb still would've gone off, and it still would've been Beau who didn't survive."

He didn't comment. Couldn't. He was turned upside down. Lost in that fog again.

Barry cleared his throat. "You and Beau met a little over a year ago when Beau got his orders to join your division. He couldn't believe it when he saw you. He e-mailed me pictures because of how much the two of you looked alike. I've got them, and a few others of you and Beau together."

"Why didn't you show them to me?"

"Because the docs said things had to be introduced slowly over time. You were remembering events from your childhood and healing fast, but I couldn't pull out those pictures, pictures of someone who could've been your twin."

"But you could lie to me for weeks?"

"I've been watching out for you for weeks, just like I would've wanted your father to do for Beau if the situation was reversed."

"I'm supposed to be happy you let my family think I'm dead?" The quiet of the small house closed in on him. How could Barry have done that? How could he have let things go on? Did he have any clue what kind of mess he'd caused by not telling the truth?

"I didn't want to, but it— The mix-up had already happened. I didn't want to cause you any more pain than you were already in. I put you first, Jack. Not the son that I couldn't bring back, *you.* The doctors—"

"Weren't the ones having to wake up and realize their life has been a lie!"

Barry rubbed his hand over his head. "I told that girl to stay away from you, I warned you and tried to keep you too busy to notice her."

"Stop blaming this on Marley. If you'd told us the truth—"

"You wouldn't have handled it any better than you are now! That's the bottom line, Jack. You think it couldn't have been worse? What do you think the press will do when they hear of a military mix-up of dead and injured soldiers? Think they'll leave you alone? Do you think they would let us deal with this privately or give you a chance to remember on your own?"

He hit the hutch with his injured hand. "You still should've told *me.* It's my life!"

Barry held his hands out in front of his body, the gesture pleading. "I did what I thought was right, what I thought was best for you and your recovery. Son, you have to understand I hadn't spent more than a few days with Beau in *years.* He stayed on base or with a girlfriend when he got leave. He didn't come home because he wanted to party with his friends. It wasn't until he met up with you that he…he started sending me e-mails. He told me how you two would play pool or cards and you'd talk about your dad. That got Beau thinking about things, about his youth and all the trouble he'd been in. He straightened up some, didn't party as much. The boy who barely spoke to me wrote me two-page e-mails.

"We couldn't talk face-to-face to save our lives, but thanks to you and finding out what it was like not to have the family support that *he* had, we kept the Internet hot. Things changed between us. You helped us, Jack, and when I realized you weren't Beau—" His shoulders straightened. "I couldn't bring my son back, but I could damn well help the man who'd given a little bit of my son back to me before he was taken away."

"What about *my* family? You don't think they'd care that I'm not *dead?*" He flinched when Barry put his hand on his shoulder.

"Jack, according to Beau, you were dead to them already."

He stilled, didn't breathe. "What's that supposed to mean?"

"Son, you were more estranged from your family than I ever was from Beau. I know they think you're dead, and I hated having to let them go on thinking that, but knowing the things Beau told me about—"

"What?"

Barry inhaled deeply, a frown on his face. "Beau told me you didn't even want to list your father as your next of kin. He said you did, but you told him you only did it so he'd be forced to acknowledge your existence in your death. Son, I kept quiet because until you're ready to go back there and face everything, what else could I do? I wasn't going to ship you off to a place I knew you didn't want to be, whether you remembered it or not."

So he had no one. Nowhere to go. No one to care. Marley's image flashed in his mind but he shoved it away. *No one.*

He stalked across the floor, found himself in front of the door taking deep, gulping breaths that didn't help. "Do you know who Joe is?"

Barry followed him, the man's footsteps dragging like stones. "Joe's your older brother. According to Beau, he's the reason why you left home. Why you never went back. Joe killed his daughter and you got tired of your father defending him."

CHAPTER EIGHTEEN

HE STARED DOWN at the headline splashed across the paper. Baby Killer Transferred to New Prison.

"Put that down and eat your breakfast." Pop glared at him. "Go get ready for school."

"I'm not going to school." He wouldn't. Any time the prison system transferred Joe or even if somebody at the paper wrote an article on babies, everybody started talking again. Not that they ever stopped.

"Yes, you are. We're going to go about our business like—"

"Like Joe didn't kill the baby?"

"He didn't."

"Then why was he convicted?" He tossed the paper aside.

"It was a mistake. You know it was."

"No, I don't."

Pop looked up from his cereal bowl. "Watch your mouth. Don't be talking about something you know nothing about."

"Fine, you want to know what I know? I know Sarah Peterson won't go to the prom with me because of Joe, neither will Julie or Samantha."

"It's just a dance."

"I don't even want to go to the dance. I'd just like for people to shut up and quit comparing me to Joe! Pop, please, I graduate in a couple weeks. Let's move. Let's take off and go somewhere else. It doesn't have to be far—"

"No! We're not taking the coward's way out. Not when your brother's innocent."

"He's in prison! He's not innocent!"

"We're not leaving."

He surged out of his chair. "Well, I am. I'm sick of this. I'm sick of living like outcasts because Joe couldn't control his temper! I'm sick of the girls not being able to date me because their parents are afraid I'll hurt *them!"*

"It's not that bad."

"It is *that bad! I've told you that!"*

"You heard me, boy. We're not moving. Now, hurry it up before you miss the bus."

Tears burned his eyes but he wouldn't let them fall. He was so sick and tired of this. "I'm leaving, Pop. My grades aren't great, but I'll graduate and when I do—I'm out of here. Come with me."

His father raised his head and stared at him, disappointment written on his face in the lines and wrinkles and the dark circles under his eyes. "If you don't believe in this family anymore then you're not a part of it. You want to leave, leave."

Something inside Jack snapped. It was like a rope holding an anvil over his head. One big hit and then everything came back in a rush, his life playing in front of his eyes at the speed of light. Too much. Too fast.

He cradled his head in his palms and moaned at the stomach-churning wave of nausea that came with the surge. Joe. Pop—his *real* father, not Barry. He remembered them. Josie. Baby Josie. Melissa, Josie's mom, and Hal, Melissa's dad. One by one their images stabbed through his head. The newspaper articles, the TV crews and the nightmare of his life appearing frequently on the six o'clock news.

"The docs said it would be best to let you remember on your own. You know that, but I talked to your shrink once I realized. He was supposed to be talking to you about *Jack*. I'd hoped that, even if you thought you were Beau, you might remember things about yourself. That way when you realized what happened..."

Mixed-up. Everything was so damned mixed-up. Images blasted him from every direction. Standing in the moon-shadowed doorway of the little house, he felt the sand and grit and blazing sun of Iraq. A radio playing in the background. Laughter. Christmases spent with guys he trusted, not the father he'd left behind because no matter what he did, Pop defended Joe, *chose* Joe, over him. Over moving on and actually having a life.

He moaned softly, rubbed his eyes with his palm, his head imploding. Barry's voice reached him, rough pats landed on his shoulder. Whispers that it would be all right. Nothing was all right. The vortex sucked him down, blindsiding him with the things he should've done, said. Never the person people needed him to be.

Pop. Barry. Marley, too. First he'd been accused of Joe's sins, now Beau's. No one here, not Marley, not her family, would ever look at him and not see Beau. And Pop—

Where was his father now? What had happened to him? There were too many questions to consider. Too much anger to deal with.

"Jack, do you remember what happened? Anything about—about Beau's last days?"

The pain in Barry's voice made him close his eyes, concentrate. Standing there in the doorway, he stayed quiet and still until things took shape. Camp. Wiring the various buildings and getting power going again.

An image separated itself from the others, slowly beginning to form in his head. Beau. Laughing, always on the lookout for a good time. It all seemed so clear now. "He had a date." The fuzzy edges sharpened, until a rough laugh tumbled out of him. He remembered his friend, his buddy, the guy who'd become his brother in all the ways that matter. "He had a date."

Barry let out a tear-filled laugh and squeezed his shoulder. "That sounds like him."

Lowering his head, he nodded. "He'd been after this girl for a while, asking her out, flirting with her like crazy. She turned him down every time and it drove him nuts. That girl kept him hopping and Beau—I think she could've been the one for him." The way Marley had been the one for him.

But not anymore.

Another rough laugh escaped Barry. "I'll be…I didn't think he'd ever find a girl he'd like that much."

He nodded, the pieces coming together faster, easier. "She finally said yes, but he had duty. We figured we'd get busted, but he checked the schedule and a couple of new guys were working. They didn't know us well enough to tell the difference."

Barry exhaled, the sound rough. "So you switched places. It wasn't the military's fault."

No, it wasn't. He didn't remember much more than that. Leaving the building side by side, both of them edgy. Beau excited about the girl, him giving Beau lectures on not blowing things with his date by acting too cocky. They'd approached the center of the camp by the mess hall. And then—nothing. Had he seen Beau die? "We switched places," he confirmed, his gut tight. "We couldn't have been more than a few feet apart when the bomb exploded."

"It wouldn't have mattered, Jack. The uniform, the tags. It still would've been Beau."

He shrugged Barry's hand off his shoulder.

"Jack?"

"I'll get Beau's truck back to you soon."

"Where are you going? Jack?"

"I'm not the son you want."

He ran outside and climbed into Beau's Dodge. As he backed out of the drive, the image of Barry standing silhouetted on the porch of the little house matched the image he had of Pop doing the same thing. Standing there, watching him drive away because he couldn't handle the pressure of being compared to someone else.

Fifteen minutes later, he rolled to a stop along the

street in front of Marley's business. She was the last person who'd take him in under the circumstances, but he owed her an explanation, however unbelievable. He could leave the truck there. She'd see to it Barry got it back.

But he'd already crawled through the alley and Clay's Jeep was parked beside Marley's truck, Angel's flashy sports car on the other side.

No way would he make it inside the apartment with Marley's defenders in place. *What would he say if he did?*

Maybe the wrong guy *had* lived.

A flash caught his attention. The second-floor apartment lights had been on, but now they were off. Moments passed, and he waited, hoping. No one left the alley. Clay and Angel were spending the night, keeping her company. Staying behind to protect her.

Good friends did that. Family did that.

He hadn't. Maybe he wouldn't have abandoned Marley the way Beau had, but…he'd abandoned his father. And to his eyes there wasn't much of a difference.

Funny how time and life experiences could change a person's outlook. Barry wasn't his father, but he'd stood by him when he had to have been torn apart by his son's death. He thought of the days Barry had spent in bed after the fish incident and now knew why. Barry had been mourning his son, then he'd set grief aside and forced himself to cope with what had happened. So that he could protect them all from a melee of press and people.

Jack stared at the window a long moment, then slid the truck into gear. Some people deserved second chances.

But he wasn't one of them.

BARRY BUCHANAN stood in her doorway looking very much like a man who'd spent the night tossing and turning.

"Is he all right?" The question tumbled out of her mouth before she could stop it even though her mind called her every kind of a fool for caring.

Barry's shoulders slumped even more. "You mean, he's not here?"

Marley shook her head, aware of Angel joining her in the living room. Clay was in the shower. They'd both spent the night. Angel for support and a friendly shoulder, Clay in the hopes that Beau's imposter would return so that he could tear him limb from limb. One glance at her face and he'd known what had happened. Clay had been biding his time ever since, giving her all manner of looks from sympathy to brotherly disappointment to out-and-out fury.

How could a woman sleep with a man thinking he was someone else?

It was yet another soap-opera moment. She felt cheap. Easy. The naive girl who'd tried so hard to grow up had obviously failed.

"I need to talk to you, Ms. Pierce."

"Now's not a good time and…I don't know where B—where he is."

"Jack." Barry lifted a shaky hand and ran it over his balding head. "His name is Jack, not Beau. You were right about that."

"You *knew?* You knew and you went along with the joke?"

"It wasn't a joke." Tears brightened the man's eyes and it was obvious it wasn't the first time that day it had happened. "Beau—my son—was killed in the bombing that injured Jack. They were friends and they… It's complicated."

Angel took her arm and pulled her out of the way. "Then why don't you come in and explain it, Mr. Buchanan." Angel directed them both to sit down on the couch, the pillow and sheet Clay had used the night before in a pile nearby. Angel had slept with her in the queen-sized bed, handing her tissues and listening the way she always had growing up.

"What's he doing here?" Clay asked, hurrying into the room. Dressed in the same clothes he'd worn last night, his shirt stuck to his wet skin and water dripped from his hair. He must've heard Barry's voice and come running thinking it was—Jack.

"That's what we're about to find out," Angel murmured, casting Marley a worried look when she remained silent. "Mr. Buchanan says he can explain."

Barry took a deep breath, met her gaze briefly and then started talking, having to backtrack several times so they could get the story straight. Before long they knew the details of the unbelievable events.

"I'm sorry for your loss, for what happened. That

must've been— How horrible." Marley pressed her hand to her mouth and tried to comprehend it all.

The saying was that everyone had a twin somewhere but…imagine finding each other. In a war, no less where thousands upon thousands worked and fought day in and day out. Becoming friends, buddies. *Imagine a woman falling for them both.*

It was surreal. Beau had been a teenage crush that shouldn't have been, but Jack—

Barry gave her brother a wary glance and stood. "I'd appreciate it if you keep this quiet for now. I need to find him. Make sure he's okay. Then we'll deal with the mix-up and get things straightened out." Barry's gaze fastened onto hers. "He didn't mean to hurt you. I can vouch for that. He was torn up last night, hated himself for not remembering."

"I should've figured it out sooner. Now that I know, I see so many differences. Beau was…Beau," she stated drily, unwilling to hurt Barry after everything that had happened. "But Jack—"

"Is a good man." Barry's gaze remained steady on hers. "Jack is everything a father should be proud of and when I remembered that Jack's father didn't want him around—"

"What do you mean? What do you know about Brody's family?" Clay asked.

"I know his brother's in jail for murder. Jack's father took the other boy's side of things and in doing so, he turned the whole town against them. Beau said Jack had a rough time of it in school. Got beat up, made fun of. The things kids do."

Angel rubbed her hand along Marley's back. "People can be cruel. They single someone out and suddenly you can't win the battle no matter how hard you try. Adults are cruel enough, but kids are vicious. High school was hell for me because of my mom, but at least she hadn't killed anyone. Can you imagine what was said to him?"

She could. Not the words necessarily, but the tone. The sneers and smirks. The looks on their faces as he walked by them, just like the expressions she'd seen after her pregnancy had become public. Marley listened as the conversation continued, but her mind was slow to process things.

Over the years all she'd ever thought of was what had happened to her. How Beau had treated her. How losing the baby had affected her. How Mama hadn't been there for her. Her, her, her. But after Barry's comments, she realized she'd acted the same way Beau had. She'd put herself first.

What had been said to her mother? What had been done?

"There aren't many people who would've set their own feelings aside to take care of Jack the way you did," Angel told Barry. "A lot of people would've immediately raised a stink about what happened regardless of the problems or health risks it posed to Jack."

"When you care for someone you put him first." Marley tried to smile, but couldn't. "You made the right decision for Jack."

Just as she had to make the decision for her mother.

Putting it off wasn't changing anything. She wasn't getting better.

"Thanks for coming and explaining things. We'll keep an eye out for him, and keep this quiet. If you find him, I'm sure Marley would like to know he's safe."

Angel's voice pulled her from her thoughts. Marley raised her head and blinked as she saw Angel and Clay walking Barry to the door. She stood and went into the bedroom, hurrying to pull on clothes.

Jack's mind had shut down to protect him, cutting off his memories until he was able to cope, but her mother didn't have that escape hatch. Instead she took pills and welcomed the cessation they offered. But what about now? Jack remembered, had come out of it, whereas her mother was…

An addict.

She couldn't do anything about Jack until he returned. *If* he returned. Her heart thumped hard in her chest and missed a beat at the thought of never seeing him again, but she ignored the sensation and grabbed a sweatshirt. Shoes. Her coat was by the door. She could only deal with one problem at a time.

She might not be able to do anything about Jack, but she had to go see her mom. Had to talk to her.

A soft knock sounded on the door. "You okay?" Angel asked, opening it far enough to poke her head inside the room.

"Yeah."

"You sure? Clay left for work. I thought you might want to talk some more. Pretty amazing story, isn't it?"

"Yeah, it is. Can you watch the shop? Open up and

stay until Amy comes? I'm going to be a while, probably all day."

Angel's eyebrows rose. "Sure, but what about Jack?"

"If he calls will you give him my cell number? I've got to go." She slid past Angel in the hall and grabbed her coat. "We'll talk later. Angel—" she turned and hugged her friend tight "—thank you."

"For what?"

"Being you. You never once said a word about what I did with…Jack."

Angel laughed her throaty laugh. "Hey, you've gotta ride those horses when you can."

Marley rolled her eyes and laughed, blushed, then hurried out the door. Exactly six minutes later she arrived at her parents' house. Marley noted her father was gone and knew he was probably working his way through another Saturday. Whatever it took to escape the problems at home.

She used her key to unlock the door, searched the bottom floor to no avail. Her mother used to get up at the crack of dawn to watch the sunrise. Now she slept the day away. "Mama?"

She climbed the stairs two at a time and found her mother in bed, propped up by pillows in a sitting position but asleep all the same. Her father had apparently brought up a tray for her. Tea and toast. Untouched. "Mama. Mama, wake up."

Her mother's lashes lifted drowsily. "Marley?"

"We need to talk."

She turned her head back and forth on the bed in short, lazy motions. "Not now, Marley, I'm tired."

"No, now." Inhaling deeply, she shook her mother's arm, jostling her roughly. "*Now,* Mama. Mama? Wake up!" She grabbed hold of the blankets and sheet and yanked them from the bed. "Come on, we're eating breakfast downstairs."

Her mother curled onto her side. "I'm not hungry."

Her words slurred a bit, her lashes rising high enough to give Marley a look at her mother's medicated gaze. How many pills did it take to make the world disappear?

Marley dragged her mother's legs over the side of the bed. "*Up.*" With a lot of pulling, pushing and prodding, Marley got her mother on her feet, dressed, then practically carried her downstairs into the kitchen. Surprisingly it wasn't as difficult as it should've been due to the weight her mother had lost.

Next came food. Marley put her mother in a chair at the kitchen table and hurriedly made instant oatmeal. More tea. Her mother sat slumped over the table, but at least her eyes were open.

"Marley, please. I'm not hungry."

"You either eat it or I'll feed you, every bite."

Her mother stiffened, looking more alert with every second that passed. She straightened. "Don't talk to me that way."

Marley put the bowl of oatmeal on the table and crossed her arms over her chest. Her mother hesitated only a second before she took a bite. It was a slow process, but gradually she lifted the spoon over and over until most of the oatmeal was gone. As if her body had wanted food, recognized its hunger. When she'd sipped the last of the tea, Marley decided she couldn't put off the inevitable.

"Come on. Let's go outside."

Her mother balked. "No. Absolutely not."

"Why? We'll only be in the backyard and it's not too cold for a walk. Unless you're afraid someone might see you with me?"

"Marley…" She looked away. "Don't say things like that."

Marley smacked her hands down onto the table, jarring the silk flower arrangement atop it and startling her mother so badly she jumped.

"Why not say it? It's true, isn't it?"

CHAPTER NINETEEN

MARLEY LEANED LOWER, closer to her. "Come on, Mama, be honest. Is it true?"

"I don't know what you're talking about."

"I think you do. Your friends talked about me and the pregnancy. Behind your back, maybe even in front of you. They probably pretended to worry and fuss, but what they said wasn't always nice, was it? And there I was. Angry, belligerent, so wrapped up in what was happening to me, that I didn't give any thought to how you might feel."

"I want to go back to bed. You should go."

"Mama, I understand now. And I'm sorry for how people treated you when it was my fault I was pregnant in the first place. That wasn't right and I'm sorry you suffered for something I did."

"You should leave, Marley."

"No! We are going to talk about this. We're going to start over, put this behind us once and for all a-and get a clean slate!" She used Jack's words deliberately, reminding herself that she and her mother both had to forgive in order to move on.

Her mother stood shakily, holding on to the table,

her skin so pale it looked translucent. "Goodbye, Marley."

"Mama, why are you doing this to yourself? It isn't fixing anything. All you're doing is missing out on your life. What about that cookbook you always wanted to put together for the church? The scrapbooking club you wanted to start? It was five years ago and, yeah, a lot has happened since then, but you can't keep drugging yourself in an attempt to hide from reality!"

She sucked in a sharp breath. "I'm doing no such—"

"You are! You know you are, otherwise you wouldn't look so guilty!"

Her mother's mouth opened and closed twice before she found the words. "You know nothing about how I feel, Marley. *Nothing.* If you did, you wouldn't—" Her mother broke off but kept walking, out of the kitchen and into the hall, head down, shoulders slumped.

"I wouldn't what?" Determined, Marley raced past her, up the stairs and into the bedroom, hearing her mother's calls for her to stop. To get out of her room and leave her alone. Marley yanked open the nightstand drawer, finding the stash of pills. How could something so small alter someone's life so easily?

She met her mother at the halfway point on the stairs.

"Marley Renee, what are you— *Give me that!*"

"No." Marley hugged the container to her chest and kept going, down the stairs, back into the kitchen.

Her mother hurried after her. "Marley, stop this!

This is— It's nonsense. Do you hear me? You have no idea what you're talking about! Give me back my medication. It's none of your concern!"

"Why isn't it in the cabinet? Why were you hiding it?"

"I wasn't!"

"You hide it because you take too much, and you started taking it after I lost the baby. It is my concern because it's your crutch for a problem—*me.*"

"No, Marley, you're not a problem!"

She waited until her mother had almost caught up with her before she stepped through the French doors into the sunshine, hardening her heart against the guilt she felt at causing her mother more pain.

She forced herself to keep going until she sat down on the step of the old playhouse, well aware of her mother watching her from inside, pacing the floor and wringing her hands.

This was it. Either her mother came out after her and the medication and acknowledged the problem or— *Or she had another breakdown?*

No. She was better now. Stronger, just like Jack.

Oh, Jack, wherever you are, be safe. She couldn't add more to the prayer because she was afraid to. Afraid if she did, she'd hope too much.

With a small cry, her mother stumbled out into the sunshine, squinting at the brightness like a cave dweller. Crying, she glared at Marley and tried to pry the box from her arms.

"Let me have it. Why are you *doing* this?"

"Because I love you." She swallowed, the lump in

her throat making it difficult. "Mama, look at me." She tightened her grip when her mother tried harder to yank the container away, but after years of self-abuse she was too weak. "Mama, please—*look at me.* What are you doing? Right now, think about it, what are you doing? Why are you so desperate to get this box? What does it mean to you?"

"Be quiet and give me—"

"You'll come outside for your *drugs,* but you won't come outside to be with me? You won't fight for the family? For *us? What are you doing?*"

Her mother's face revealed the naked truth. Her fear and dawning awareness. She fell to her knees, her bid for the box over even though she still held on to it. She started to sob and like a child seeking comfort, slid her arms around Marley and held tight, the box between them a sad, sorry replacement for the baby that should've been.

"I'm sorry. Oh, Marley, I failed you."

Marley set the box aside, out of reach, and hugged her mother close. "It wasn't your fault. I got pregnant, but you… *You* raised me the best you could. You taught me so much, but I was the one who didn't listen." Marley framed her mother's face with her hands, forcing her to look at her. "No one should have judged you because of me, and I'm sorry you felt the need to escape by—by taking the pills."

Fresh tears filled her mother's gaze and trickled over her wrinkled cheeks. "Oh, Marley, it wasn't—it wasn't that. People talked, yes, but I—I understood. People do that sort of thing."

She stared at her, confused. If not that, what? "Then why? Mama, why are you taking them?"

Her mother remained silent, seemed to go inside herself.

"Mama, whatever it is, you can tell me."

"I can't."

"You *can*. Please, tell me, please. I can't help you unless you try to help yourself. Talk to me. Whatever it is, you can tell me."

Her mother shook from head to toe, her head moving back and forth like a robot. "It's…it's… I took them because of what was wrong with *me*."

"What's wrong with you?"

She lowered her lashes, her expression one of utter shame. "I take them to try to be better."

"Better how? Mama, it wasn't your fault."

"But it was. Marley…I thought horrible things. Mean, shameful things about the baby because I saw you getting bigger and…I didn't want it. I didn't want you to have to live with the reminder of that man and how he'd treated you. I knew the problems you'd face trying to raise it alone and I thought you would be better off if it didn't exist. Oh, Marley, don't you see? I might as well have pushed you down those steps myself."

Marley tried to set aside her shock and get inside her mother's head. Realized that to do so, she had to think from within a depressive state, one of sadness and upset and anxiety. Fear. "So when I lost the baby, you believed it happened because you thought about it? *Mama.*"

A ragged wail tore from her mother's mouth before she clamped a hand over her lips. She nodded, crying, her head low. "I didn't want it and I sat there in that chair by your hospital bed thinking it might be best if something happened to it. Then the doctor came in and told you. Marley, you screamed. You *screamed,* and I felt it all the way to my soul. You wanted that baby because you *loved* her and didn't want to lose her. And there I'd sat thinking those horrible things. I did that, it was my fault."

Depression can last years. With medication, it was manageable but still people suffered and her mother had gone from not taking any medicine at all to overdosing on it. So many things made sense. "It's not your fault."

"You're wrong. It is. What kind of person thinks those things? How could I feel that way about my own grandchild? Marley, I couldn't…I couldn't *look at you* and not remember the pain I caused you, and my guilt… I just wanted to get better."

Marley wrapped her arms around her mother and held her, surrounded by weeds and leaves, the cloudy December sky rolling over their heads. She'd known perfectly well how badly she'd embarrassed the family by coming home pregnant and unwed. And as upsetting as it was to know her mother's darkest thoughts, how could she blame her for not wanting the baby when *she* hadn't wanted her? Not in the beginning.

"I didn't want the baby, either." The words came out slow, painfully honest. "If you're to blame for what happened, Mama, then so am I, because I didn't want her, either, not at first." She closed her eyes and tried to remember the amazement she'd felt that long-ago day. "Then I felt her move. I loved her with all my heart because I knew she had spunk."

Her comment earned a tearful laugh from her mother. "She would've been like you." Her mother's shoulders began to quake with renewed tears.

"I wanted so badly to be a good mother. To be like *you,* Mama. I wanted to make everything okay since I'd screwed up the beginning of her life, but just when I realized how very much I loved her…she was gone."

Her mother raised her head, her gaze bleak.

"Mama, I slipped on the steps. That's all. And if she—if my baby girl was meant to be with us right now, she would be. I believe that. I believe that with all my heart, don't you?"

More tears appeared.

Marley smoothed a hand over her mother's hair, remembering when she was little and how the feel of her mother's hands stroking her hair made her feel so safe. "Mama, there is no doubt in my mind that if I'd had the baby and she were alive today, you'd be in there with her showing her how to make cookies or reading a story, doing whatever you could so that she didn't feel neglected by her father. You're too good of a person to have treated her any differently."

"I'd like to hope so but—"

"No buts," she stated firmly. "No buts. It's not in you to be mean. You are not to blame, Mama. You were more willing to hurt yourself taking all those pills than to risk hurting your family again. But that has to stop. Mama, I need you. I *need* you so bad right now because there's so much going on, but I need you *awake* with a clear head a-and able to hear me so that you can help me."

Her mother's lips parted. "Marley. Honey, what is it? What's wrong?"

That was the mother she knew. In her mother's eyes Marley finally saw the love that had been buried beneath a mountain of guilt and shame for far too many years.

She shook her head and forced a smile. It was too soon to tell her mother everything about Beau and Jack. And considering how the truth had become known... Maybe one day she'd tell her the story, but not now. If Jack came back, if things worked out, she'd introduce her mother to *Jack,* no one else.

"I just need you. I've tried to be patient and give you time, and I'm sorry if it seems selfish, but I need you so please, please, let me help you. You don't need the pills, you don't need to feel guilty."

"Oh, Marley. I'm okay, it's just—"

"You're not okay. You've taken them too long, grown too dependent. But together we can do anything, and you can stop taking them. We'll go to a doctor and see about what to do next. We'll take it slow, a day at a time. An hour at a time if we have to." Marley laughed softly, and indicated the weeds where they sat. "We'll pull them all, we'll decorate the house for Christmas, every room, the outside, too. You used to love white lights on the shrubs. We'll do it together. I'll be here for you every step, but you have to decide—*right now*—which is more important to you—the pills, or your family? Mama, you *have* to decide because if I…if I fall in love with someone and we have a baby, I want her to know you and to love you the way I love you. But you *can't* be like you are now."

Tears flowing, her mother didn't move. She kept her head down, but Marley saw her gaze shift to the box sitting so near.

"We all want to feel good, and after everything that happened… But you don't need that stuff. Not all of it. Not anymore. Because we're okay now. Right?"

Hope warred with fear. Her mother swallowed. "You forgive me?"

"Yes. *Yes.* Mama, please, I just want you to come back to me."

"Your father, oh, your father won't understand. I—I hid them. He doesn't know about—about all of them. He doesn't know."

He did. He had to, but her father hadn't known how to fix the problem, so he'd ignored it, hoped she'd get better on her own. "He loves you. He didn't want you to hurt anymore. We'll do this together, all of us. The way a family should. But you have to be the one to decide."

Silence. Her mother inhaled deeply. Wiped her face and lowered her head, shed more tears as her lips moved silently. Then…then she smiled. "Yes. With God's help and yours, I can do this."

JACK ROLLED OVER onto his back and stared up at the ceiling of the dingy motel room. The walls shook as a train sped by mere feet away from the back of the building, but the rumble of the tracks was strangely comforting. At least now he could remember why.

The little house he'd shared with Joe and Pop had been a few acres from the tracks, but the sounds of the big locomotives could be heard. Normal no matter what time of the day or night.

He turned again, rolling off the bed to his feet. The bathroom mirror was clean but spotted with age, the caulk around the sink yellowed. He washed his face in the cold tap water, then glared at the reflection staring back.

His gut tightened with regret-filled nausea. When he'd left Taylorsville, he'd vowed never to go back and he'd kept the promise. And even though he'd picked up the phone countless times throughout the years and dialed, he'd hung up before it could ring through.

After meeting Beau he'd finally gotten the courage to call. Dialing the number had been hard, but harder still was the sound of the recorded voice stating that the number was no longer in service. Pop wouldn't have left Taylorsville while Joe was still in prison. If he was still alive, he'd changed the number deliberately, making it impossible for the son who'd run away to call home.

Because it wasn't home.

Ted Brody had defended Joe with every breath in his body. He wouldn't listen to the proof, denied what was being said by the townspeople and didn't care what was happening with Jack because Joe was always foremost in his mind. He'd tried to pass it off as sibling jealousy, but it was way more than that. It was the energy that went into Joe's case, Joe's problems, Joe's life—when he needed his father, too.

He swore and stripped off his underwear, turning on the tap and getting in the shower, all the while trying to forget the last shower he'd taken with Marley. The way she'd looked at him, the smile on her face.

Barry could've saved them all a lot of heartache if he'd only told the truth. Maybe he hadn't known right away, but when he'd figured it out he should've—

He hit the shower stall with his fist, then leaned his head against it and let the spray rain over him. He'd actually begun to think of the little house in South Ridge as home.

But now more than ever he realized he didn't have one.

CHAPTER TWENTY

"I'VE ASKED HER to marry me, you know."

Marley glanced up from the dish she scrubbed in her mother's sink and focused on Clay's not-quite-happy expression.

Her mother, father and Dr. Myners were in the dining room going over counseling options. The next few weeks would be hell, but Dr. Myners was confident that her mother would be off all except the most necessary medications by the New Year.

The Christmas frenzy would be over in a matter of days and afterward, Marley would have nearly two months to spend helping her mother rebuild her life. As terrifying as it was, she couldn't wait. Until then, her father had taken a leave of absence to stay with her mother.

"Hello? No response?"

She blinked. "What did Angel say?"

"Angel says she'll marry again when hell freezes over."

She laughed, cutting it short when she spied his expression. "Sorry."

"I don't get it. We fight, but what else is new. I actually think she uses it as a form of foreplay."

"That qualifies as too much information."

"And physically—"

"*Way* too much information," she murmured pointedly, cutting him off.

Clay inhaled and wrapped both hands around the back of his neck. "I'm just saying I don't get it."

He was asking advice from her? She was the one who'd fallen for the wrong guy. Again.

"Maybe she needs time to adjust. To find out who she is as a person. She's just taken charge of a new business and is getting things off the ground. You can't blame her for wanting space."

Clay leaned his hips against the countertop and frowned at her. "Kind of like Jack?"

She didn't want to talk about Jack. She didn't want to *think* about Jack. If she did, she'd break down and it had been a hard enough day as it was. Wondering where he was, if he was okay. *If he'd come back.*

"He's gotta be freaked out, you know? He wakes up and thinks he's Beau, begins to figure things out. Then—*wham*—he gets hit all over again." Clay shifted, his hand falling on her shoulder. "I'm just saying that if you think Angel needs time, the same applies to Jack. I feel sorry for the guy. Especially for being so nasty to him—seeing as how now I know he *wasn't* the jerk who—well, you know."

That she did.

"Look, I'll come by here again later tonight. There's something I've got to do."

"Going to go see Angel?"

Clay opened his mouth to respond, then shut it

again. "No. I said I'd back off some and I will. I'm heading into work for a while. Something's bugging me and I can't stop thinking about it so I'm going to go check it out." He dropped a kiss on her head. "Quit worrying. He'll come back."

Maybe. But if he did, would Jack want to build a relationship with her after everything that happened? What man wanted to always feel like a stand-in for someone else?

JACK DROVE BACK into South Ridge in the early hours of Wednesday morning. He'd stayed at the cheap motel the whole time he'd been gone. Bought pizza and sandwiches from a fast-food place nearby and went over everything in his head until his cash ran out and he had to make a decision. The bottom line became clear after the anger wore off.

Barry had done for him what a father should've done, and for that he had to be grateful.

After learning the truth about Beau's death, Barry had to have died a little more inside every time he'd called him Beau. But instead of being bitter, Barry had kept up the charade and put his mental and physical health first. Something his own father hadn't done because the man had focused on Joe to the exclusion of everything else.

But knowing how much it would hurt Barry to look at him and remember what he'd lost... He had to go back, just long enough to let Barry know how grateful he was and tell him he appreciated Barry being the father he'd needed. Then he'd leave.

Without seeing Marley? Pain sliced into him at the thought, but it couldn't be helped.

Jack turned onto the highway and headed toward the little house. Marley didn't want to see him. Why would she? She had to be feeling used, angry. She believed he'd tricked her, seduced her in order to play some kind of twisted game. He hated that she'd consider him capable of that, but why wouldn't she? The past they'd had together was no more—a good thing in itself—but with it gone, they had…

A clean slate.

He stilled. Would she see it that way? Would Marley ever be able to look at him and see a future, not a reminder of the past and the pain Beau had caused?

Anger filled him. He cared for Marley way more than a passing fling. Her smile, her softness. That wild-looking hair. Marley could be cynical and contrary, but she was also sweet and kind and beautiful. She'd never be boring. And he liked the idea of always knowing how she felt by simply looking into her expressive face. She'd tell him straight up what she liked, hated, wanted, and not leave him guessing. Honesty was such a turn-on, and he loved that.

Jack thumped his hand against the steering wheel. He didn't love her. He could like her all he wanted, but it wouldn't change anything. There weren't going to be any Christmas miracles for him because whatever Marley had felt for him, she'd felt it thinking he was *Beau.* He might have been able to forget his past, but no way could he allow himself to forget that.

He pulled into the driveway of the little rental, but

Barry's truck was gone. Inside, he turned on the lights and looked around, remembering when boredom had him hating the ugly wallpaper. Now it felt like home. Jack turned to go when he spotted something atop the kitchen table. A note?

Don't leave without saying goodbye—that's an order.

It was signed "Pop."

He gathered up the envelope of pictures under the note and carried them with him into the living room. Sitting in Barry's favorite recliner, he looked through the photos of him and Beau together, smiling, remembering. Mourning his cocky but loyal friend. Barry was right. Beau had been figuring things out in Iraq, had grown up while facing the reality of war.

Half an hour later the sun broke over the horizon as Jack pulled onto the road leading to the housing development. He knew Barry would already be at work, determined to do whatever it took to take his mind off the present predicament and problems.

Barry must have heard him drive up because he came out of the house, his face pale, circles under his eyes. Jack stared at the older man, trying to guard against the pain.

Straightening his shoulders, Barry pulled something from his back pocket and headed toward him. "Thank God you're back. Are you okay?" He tugged Jack into his arms and pounded him on the back.

When Barry let go, Jack stepped back and leaned

against the truck for support. Saying what he had to say wasn't going to be easy, neither was leaving. He indicated Beau's truck. "Thanks for not calling the cops on me for borrowing this."

"I wouldn't do that to you."

"And for taking care of me. You put me first and kept your feelings for Beau buried so that I— I'm glad you did what you did, that you didn't send me back there after you found out. Thank you."

Barry nodded, his expression solemn.

"Did you call the military yet?"

"I didn't want to until I knew you'd be okay with it."

How could he be ready to face the fallout? He just hoped charges weren't filed against him. As bad as a dishonorable discharge would be, prison would be worse. His mind laughed at him. He'd be just like Joe. There was a twisted irony in that. "It's fine. I know you want to get Beau's body moved. It'll need to be done soon."

"He's at peace, Jack. When the time's right, it'll happen. You're the one who needs to be ready for it all. Have you been in contact with Dr. Steinman?"

"No."

"You should go see him." Barry lost more color, the paper crunching in his hands when he squeezed it. "Before you thank me for not sending you back, you need to see these."

Jack hesitated before accepting the sheaf of papers.

"Marley brought them by yesterday evening. Her brother did some research and… You need to read it, Jack."

His heart thumped in his chest. If this was an

obituary for his father he'd— "Oh, God." Brody Declared Innocent After Release From Prison. "He was innocent? They sent him to prison and he was *innocent?*"

"Your father was right."

Jack walked to the end of the truck bed. *Innocent?*

"We've all made mistakes, Jack. You weren't the only one who didn't believe him. How do you think those jurors feel knowing they sent him to prison?"

He stared down at the picture of Joe. His brother was unsmiling, looking as though he tolerated the camera for the sake of the woman beside him. His…fiancée. The article was nearly three years old, which meant by now they were probably married and— Where was Pop? He scanned the article but saw no mention of Ted Brody anywhere. "Joe said he didn't do it. Pop said Joe didn't do it. I hated them both for lying. I *hated* him for pretending it wasn't true. Pop took Joe's side when everyone in town, everyone including me— *Dammit!*" He crushed the paper in his hands.

"Are you mad because he's innocent—or because you were wrong?"

Jack didn't answer. He was angry because everything was so screwed up. He sighed, his breath emerging as a white cloud in the cold morning air.

"What happens now, Jack?"

"I don't know."

"Yeah, you do. It's time to go home, son. Do you want the military having to explain why they're digging up that grave, or are you man enough to spare them the pain of having a soldier on their doorstep a second time? What do you think they're going to feel if they're told you're alive but you're not there to see them?" Barry put his hand on Jack's shoulder and turned him around to face him. "If they can see your face, know you're alive, all the anger and resentment and everything else? Those will just disappear."

"How can you be sure? You either believe in the family or you're not a part of it, that's what Pop said. I didn't believe in either one of them, especially Joe."

Barry's expression, the pain in his eyes, was hard to look at. "Your father may have said it, but he didn't mean it. Do you have any idea how many things I said to Beau in anger that I didn't mean? That I wish I could take back? Your father didn't mean it, son. You had more pride than brains, and he was a man struggling to get up in the morning because Joe had broken his heart." Barry squeezed his shoulder. "No one knows someone else's thoughts. Your father took up for Joe, defended him, but there's no way he could've been a hundred percent sure that Joe didn't do it. Jack… I lost my only son. Right now, your father thinks he's lost one of his, the son *he drove away* because of his own blind stupidity. That's not something a man takes lightly. He's had time to think about things, knows he messed up. Just like you've had time to grow up. Let him have Christmas with his boys, Jack. You might have run away as an eighteen-year-old kid, but go home a man, one old enough to own up to your faults and willing to ask for forgiveness. You do that, and no father or brother will turn you away."

There was only one way to find out if that were true. But where was he going to find the courage to face them?

MARLEY SHOOK THE CORD in her hand with an exasperated sound. "Come on, don't do this *now.* Work!" The official ceremony announcing the winner of the Winter Festival competition was about to start. Wouldn't it just figure that half the lights on her display would go out?

"They're sold out of the white lights." Angel panted as she jogged up to the booth. "I even tried to buy a set from the car lot. That ugly tree they have in the window could use some toning down, but they refused." She pulled a boxed set of bright blue bulbs from a bag. "This was all I could get. Maybe we can make it look sort of retro and flower-powered."

"I could give you a hand."

Marley froze at the sound of the masculine voice behind her. She stared at Angel's face, watched as her friend stared at Jack with an expression full of relief before it tightened into a protective glare.

"So, you finally decided to show up?"

"Angel."

"I came to apologize."

"Well, okay, then. Get to it." Angel grinned cheekily. "And don't screw it up." Her gaze dropped to Marley's and she stared hard. "You, either."

Marley closed her eyes with a sigh, conscious of Jack's husky chuckle. A moment later he knelt beside her, close enough that she felt the brush of his knee, his hands plucking the cord from hers.

"You probably blew a fuse." He pulled the plug-ins apart and shifted so that the lights from the other displays illuminated the flat surface. Using his fingernail, he opened the tiny covering, popped the fuse out and nodded. "Where's the new set?"

Her hands shook but she somehow managed to open the box and find one of the little plastic bags of fuses and extra bulbs. Within seconds all of her lights were working.

The image she'd tried to perfect was that of a house, a window. Inside the house she'd placed a Christmas tree draped in vintage-style red, white and blue ribbon, added old-fashioned glass bulbs and tucked antique toys beneath the limbs. A weathered sleigh, a rocking horse with a fuzzy mane, baby dolls and wind-up toys, symbols of Christmases past encircled by a train. An old chair, faux mantel. Braided rug.

A clapboard wall was her "house" and the window's support. Beneath that, the foundation of her display was made up of Keystone Rock. Pretty on their own with their basket weave design. The base was heavily landscaped with lighted shrubs and ornamental trees, winter-hardy pansies and forced bulbs. An old wooden fence draped with rose hips and greenery served as her backdrop, red velvet bows placed at the arches. Her intention was to remind people of old-fashioned Christmases spent with the ones they loved.

"It looks beautiful, Marley."

"Thank you. And thanks for the—the help."

Awkward silence surrounded them, broken by the school choir singing carols on the corner.

Why was he here? Jack hadn't *been* Jack when they'd made love and even though it had meant everything to her, who knew what it meant to him? She closed her eyes and sent up a quick prayer, something she'd been doing a lot of lately as her mother began to withdraw from her medication. The road ahead wouldn't be easy, but they'd survive as a family.

"Marley? You all right?"

She kept her eyes closed and added another prayer, wondering if her imagination was overcompensating for her lack of sleep because Jack's voice had sounded so caring. Loving.

Loving?

Calloused fingertips brushed her hair from her cheek and mouth, tucking the strands behind her ear, gently turning her face until…

"Marley, look at me and tell me… Tell me you don't hate me for putting you through this. Tell me I didn't blow everything with you."

Sniffling to hold back a sudden rush of tears, she blinked and it took everything in her to keep those tears in check. "I d-don't hate you. I still can't believe it. I know you must be in shock."

"I was. I needed to think and I wasn't sure if you or Barry would want to see me again."

"I did. I—I do." Jack looked as tired and worn-out as she felt. As anxious and nervous, too. Marley pushed herself up, and he stood with her, but he didn't back away. Face-to-face, she asked, "Are you okay? Really okay?"

One side of his mouth pulled up in a sad, lopsided

grin so endearing and sexy she felt the pain inside her heal just a bit. If he was still smiling at her after all of this…

"As good as I can be, I guess. There's a lot that has to be dealt with." He glanced around and lowered his voice. "The military has to be notified so that I can be declared living. And then there's the fallout from switching tags."

"My father says they'll probably change your discharge status from Honorable to Dishonorable, but that you shouldn't be reprimanded otherwise."

"I hope not."

"It'll be okay, Jack. There are worse things that could happen than that and the people who count know how honorable you are."

"Meaning you?" He swallowed, the sound audible, when she nodded. "Marley, are you okay that it's me and not Beau?"

"You never were Beau."

Jack stiffened and started to step away, but she stopped him by grabbing the open front of his coat and holding him in place. If he went anywhere she was going with him. "You never were Beau," she repeated softly, "because from the very beginning I saw the differences in you. Jack, that's what I meant, nothing else. Am I okay with you being kind and caring and gentle and good? Yes. Is it surreal that you're all of those things and look like Beau? Most definitely, *yes.* I was so confused. I didn't understand how someone could be so different, but… That's just it. You *are* different. Totally different. You're the man he wasn't, the man Beau never could be because the boy I knew can never match up to you. *You* are…" She knew the words she wanted to say but—

"Someone you want to spend time with?"

She smiled up at him. "Definitely."

Jack was silent, his gaze searching. "Do your parents know?"

"My father does. He says he'll represent you if there are problems, or find someone who can help you if things get complicated. Don't look so surprised. I think he's relieved that you aren't Beau and wants to make up for the way he treated you that day. And my mother—I'll have to tell you about her later, but… she's going to be okay with it. I know she will be. The Pierce family have all become more understanding and enlightened to a lot of things while you've been gone."

"What about you?"

Heat slid into Marley's cheeks. She was surrounded by people who knew her parents and would no doubt be on the phone gossiping about her standing there latched on to Jack, but she didn't care. Now that he was here, she could look into his face and see that he didn't hold her past with Beau against her. "I'm okay," she whispered. "I'm okay because I love the man you are. The one who carries trees for me and—and sees me to my door to make sure I'm safe. Are you okay with me thinking at the time you were a new and improved Beau?"

Jack pressed his lips to her ear. "I don't like the

thought of you with anyone else. But you didn't know what was going on and neither did I. You love me?"

She smoothed her hand up to his jaw. "Yes," she said, aware that he hadn't said the words to her. Given all he'd been through she wasn't going to rush him. The new and improved Marley, the girl who'd grown up and learned to be a better judge of character, saw it in his eyes. Jack would tell her when he was ready. "We can take things slow. As slow as you need. You've got a lot to deal with right now and so do I, but together…"

He kissed her, a seductive meeting of lips that reflected all the need between them. A heartbeat later he deepened the caress, sweeping into her mouth with hot, sweet strokes that confirmed what she felt for him. No one had ever made her feel like this. No one.

The kiss ended and Marley gasped when she opened her eyes and saw the sparkle of tears in his gaze. He blinked twice and they were gone, but they were there. Tears for her. For them.

"You saw me, *knew* me, when I didn't know myself." Jack kissed her again. "And I love you for it. I always will." He dropped a kiss to her nose and drew away, holding out his hand. "Hi."

Bemused, Marley slowly put her palm in his. "Uh… Hi?"

"I'm Jack Brody."

Catching on, she tilted her face toward his, uncaring that from the stage, the chairperson for the competition had begun announcing the runners-up. Some things were more important. "Marley Pierce. You new to town? Maybe I can show you around sometime."

"And the winner is..."

"I can't wait." Smiling the smile that made her toes curl in her boots, Jack pulled her flush against him for another kiss. Her blood pumped quickly through her veins, and she wrapped her arms around his neck and kissed him with every ounce of love inside her.

A loud roar of applause erupted around them. Jack stiffened. She felt it, but she didn't care. He tried to end the kiss and raise his head, but she wouldn't let him.

"Marley," he murmured against her mouth, "you won."

She blinked up at him, dazed, then realized exactly what he'd said. Realized they were surrounded by laughing, clapping people, all of them giving her and Jack knowing looks and grins. Heat flooded her cheeks when she spotted Clay shaking his head at her while Angel stood beside him giving Marley a thumbs up.

"Babe, you won." Jack kissed her quickly again, then nudged her toward the stage. "Go on, go get your prize. You got what you wanted for Christmas."

Smiling, Marley ignored the heat in her cheeks and threaded her way through the crowd on wobbly knees. Climbing the steps, she glanced back, her gaze zeroing in on Jack who clapped and whistled, a broad, proud grin on his face. Her heart beat faster. "I most certainly did."

EPILOGUE

Christmas Eve...

"STOP FUSSING. Jack, you look fine."

"I should've gotten a haircut."

Marley pulled his hand down and held it in hers, stopping them halfway between the truck and the large Victorian-style house. "If you don't stop pulling at it, you're not going to have any left." She squeezed his fingers tight. "Look at me. It's going to be okay. Take a deep breath and remember what Barry said."

They'd pulled up to the B and B Joe and his wife owned a good ten minutes ago, but he hadn't worked up the courage to go inside.

The house was lit up from top to bottom in white lights. Electric candles in the windows, more white lights in the shrubs. It looked like a happy house, like a happy family lived there. Was he really ready to go in there and screw it up? "Maybe I should wait until after Christmas. Barry knows Beau isn't ever coming back, and he's feeling his loss. He could be wrong about my family. Maybe I should let the military make first contact and tell them so that they won't freak out and think they're seeing a ghost."

"They'll be happy to see you."

"What do I say? *Surprise? There's been a mistake?*"

She grimaced. "Maybe something a little less...I don't know, but not that."

"Lot of help you are."

Marley hugged his arm to her body and prodded him to get moving again. "Maybe you should just knock on the door and let whatever happens, happen."

That didn't appeal, either. He needed a plan, but what? He ran his free hand through his hair again. "I wouldn't get through this without you. You know that, right?" He squeezed the fingers that held his, knowing deep down Marley was as nervous as he was at seeing his family for the first time. "It's okay what they say to me, whatever it is." He glanced down to see Marley's expression soften.

"Jack."

"It is," he insisted. "They've got a lot of reasons not to want anything to do with me. That's up to them. I don't want you getting in the middle of things and taking up for me if it turns into a shouting match or something."

"It won't. They'll be happy to see you."

He pulled her against him, feeling like a coward and needing the feel of her to give him strength. "Marley, I'm just saying that whatever happens, I'm okay with it because I have you. Because I love you." Inhaling the scent of her hair, he felt the tension leave his body. He'd made peace with himself, with the past.

Whatever took place after they walked through that door, he had Marley and she was all he needed. Barry, too. Beau's father had offered him a partnership in the business, one he planned to take him up on so long as he could open up an office in South Ridge. "More than you'll ever know. I can face anything with you by my side."

She thumped his shoulder with her fist. "Stop it. Don't make me face them crying, it's not a pretty sight and— Oh, great."

He laughed huskily and kissed her cheek, releasing her and helping her blot the tears with his fingers. "Perfect. You look beautiful."

Marley sniffled, pulled herself together and then stood on tiptoe to kiss him. "You'll be okay. Let's just knock on the door and do this so that you'll see I'm right." She smirked. "I have been right a lot here lately."

Jack groaned at the reminder even though he prayed she was right this time, too. He stepped onto the bricked patio near the porch. "That you have. But we can't go in there yet."

She groaned. "Jack, just—"

"Something's still not right." He frowned down at her. "It's you, but don't worry, I can fix the problem."

"Stop stalling."

He pulled the box from his pocket, the one he'd planned to give her tomorrow morning. Now seemed like a better time, and he was freaked out enough by the whole scenario about to play out that he liked the idea of her wearing something he gave her when she met his father and Joe for the first time.

"What is— Oh, Jack."

"I saw this sign outside a store in town. It said this represented the journey we take with the person we love." He opened the box, the five diamonds inside linked together varying in sizes from smallest to largest and dangled from a fragile chain. "This—*us*—definitely qualifies as a journey." Marley's mouth parted as she gazed at the necklace. "Do you like it?"

"It's *beautiful.*" Tears sparkled in her eyes once more and she blinked rapidly. "Put it on me?"

Seconds later he smoothed the necklace into place at her throat, staring at the diamonds and watching them shine in the light. "Marley, why should they forget what I did? How I acted?"

She trailed her fingers over the diamonds while lifting her chin, determination and grit stamped on her face. "Because they love you. And people do stupid things. And you were *all* at fault."

He smoothed his hand over her hair, loving the feel of it. She'd worn it down and loose for him. "You understand. That's all that matters."

"No, Jack, it's—"

The door behind them opened. "Joe, do you know where we put the bag for Max's bike? I can't—"

Jack tensed and whirled around so fast one of his feet slipped on the air-dampened brick. Blood pumped past his ears in loud gushes, but it didn't drown out the sound of Marley's gasp.

Because of the woman's words, he searched the shadows of the trellised porch but didn't see anyone until he moved to the steps, Marley's hand gripped tight in his. A man stood up from where he'd sat on a porch swing, a thick blanket draped over his chest, shock apparent on his face.

Joe?

The dark-haired woman gasped when she got a good look at Jack, her gaze narrowing on him, sliding to Joe, then back to him again. She was the woman in the newspaper article, the one who'd been listed as Joe's fiancée. A wedding ring sparkled on her finger.

"Joe?"

"I don't know what's going on," his brother said in response to the question in her voice.

Jack opened his mouth, but couldn't speak. All he could do was stare at Joe. Light spilled from the open doorway, allowing him to make out his brother's features. One glance said it all. Joe was bigger, broader, tougher. Prison had taken a toll. But he looked good. Happy.

"Ashley? Don't forget about the stuff you hid in my closet. Do you want me to go get it?"

Pop. His knees turned to rubber in an instant. Pop was there? He hadn't been able to find a listing for him. If he lived there that made sense.

Jack's hand tightened on Marley's, but he didn't take his eyes off the man behind Joe's wife.

The woman—*Ashley*—stepped out onto the porch and moved to Joe's side. Pop followed. "Ashley? Do you want—"

Pop saw him and paled so quickly Jack was afraid the shock was too much for him.

Joe shifted slightly and drew his attention and for the first time he noticed the blanket Joe held was pink.

Pink. *A baby?*

Barely able to force air in and out of his chest, he had a hard time tearing his gaze away from the tiny mound of pink to look at them all again. Joe and his wife. Pop. In their faces he recognized shock, curiosity and… Relief?

His brain shut down, his throat locked up. He needed to speak, to be the first to say something, but how did a person apologize for the kind of pain he'd caused?

Fighting tears and losing the battle, his gaze shifted to the bundle of pink cradled so protectively against Joe's broad chest. How could he ever have thought Joe would hurt his baby girl?

"I'm sorry." The words emerged thick, raw, barely recognizable. He shook his head but kept his gaze on the sleeping baby, unable to look Joe or his Pop in the eyes. Ashamed that he hadn't believed in them, in the family. "I'm sorry."

Pop charged forward and Jack barely registered the sight of his father's tears before Pop pulled him into a hug, his whole body shaking.

"They said you were dead. We *buried* you."

"I know. It's a long story. I was hurt, but I'm here. Pop, I'm *sorry*."

"No. No more of that now."

"I have to say it." He buried his nose in his father's shoulder and held tight. "I should've been stronger. I'm sorry I took the coward's way out."

"You did what you had to do. I didn't mean what I said, either. But that's done now. Over, you hear me? Jack—" Pop drew back and palmed his face. "Jack, you're *home*. Praise God, you're alive!"

Smiling, he pulled Pop's hands from his cheeks and stepped back. There was more to say. He held his hand open and Marley's palm slipped into his, clasped tight in support and love as she moved to stand beside him. When he finally worked up the nerve to look at his brother, Joe's gaze was stark, full of memories and pain.

"I'm sorry. It's not enough. It'll never be enough, but I was wrong and…I should've believed in you. I should've believed in my brother. Joe, is there any way you can forgive me?"

Silence followed his words. Madonna's breathless version of "Santa Baby" played somewhere in the house, and then Angel's voice filled the air as her on-air personality, Delilah Kane. Still, Joe said nothing.

Swallowing, he accepted that as his answer. "The—" he had to stop and clear his throat "—the military will be in contact soon." He turned to walk away.

"Jack."

Marley's fingers tightened on his, squeezed hard when he didn't immediately turn around. He stared into her eyes and found the courage to face Joe again.

His brother moved close and wrapped an arm around him, pulled him to his side so that they hugged, mindful of the baby between them. "What took you so long, little brother?"

* * * * *

Brad shoved the truck into gear and drove to the bottom of the hill, where the road forked. Turn left, and he'd be home in five minutes. Turn right, and he was headed for Indian Rock.

He had no damn business going to Indian Rock.

He had nothing to say to Meg McKettrick, and if he never set eyes on the woman again, it would be two weeks too soon.

He turned right.

He couldn't have said why.

He just drove straight to the Dixie Dog Drive-In.

Back in the day, he and Meg used to meet at the Dixie Dog, by tacit agreement, when either of them had been away. It had been some kind of universe thing, purely intuitive.

Passing familiar landmarks, Brad told himself he ought to turn around. The old days were gone. Things had ended badly between him and Meg anyhow, and she wasn't going to be at the Dixie Dog.

He kept driving.

He rounded a bend, and there was the Dixie Dog. Its big neon sign, a giant hot dog, was all lit up and going through its corny sequence—first it was covered in red squiggles of light, meant to suggest ketchup, and then yellow, for mustard.

Brad pulled into one of the slots next to a speaker, rolled down the truck window and ordered.

A girl roller-skated out with the order about five minutes later.

When she wheeled up to the driver's window, smiling, her eyes went wide with recognition, and she dropped the tray with a clatter.

Silently Brad swore. Damn if he hadn't forgotten he was a famous country singer.

The girl, a skinny thing wearing too much eye makeup, immediately started to cry. "I'm sorry!" she sobbed, squatting to gather up the mess.

"It's okay," Brad answered quietly, leaning to look down at her, catching a glimpse of her plastic name tag. "It's okay, Mandy. No harm done."

"I'll get you another dog and a shake right away, Mr. O'Ballivan!"

"Mandy?"

She stared up at him pitifully, sniffling. Thanks to

the copious tears, most of the goop on her eyes had slid south. "Yes?"

"When you go back inside, could you not mention seeing me?"

"But you're Brad O'Ballivan!"

"Yeah," he answered, suppressing a sigh, "I know."

She rolled a little closer. "You wouldn't happen to have a picture you could autograph for me, would you?"

"Not with me," Brad answered.

"You could sign this napkin, though," Mandy said. "It's only got a little chocolate on the corner."

Brad took the paper napkin and her order pen, and scrawled his name. Handed both items back through the window.

She turned and whizzed back toward the side entrance to the Dixie Dog.

Brad waited, marveling that he hadn't considered incidents like this one before he'd decided to come back home. In retrospect, it seemed shortsighted, to say the least, but the truth was, he'd expected to be—Brad O'Ballivan.

Presently Mandy skated back out again, and this time she managed to hold on to the tray.

"I didn't tell a soul!" she whispered. "But Heather and Darlene *both* asked me why my mascara was all smeared." Efficiently she hooked the tray onto the bottom edge of the window.

Brad extended payment, but Mandy shook her head.

"The boss said it's on the house, since I dumped your first order on the ground."

He smiled. "Okay, then. Thanks."

Mandy retreated, and Brad was just reaching for the food when a bright red Blazer whipped into the space beside his. The driver's door sprang open, crashing into the metal speaker, and somebody got out in a hurry.

Something quickened inside Brad.

And in the next moment Meg McKettrick was standing practically on his running board, her blue eyes blazing.

Brad grinned. "I guess you're not over me after all," he said.

COMING NEXT MONTH

#1458 GOING FOR BROKE • Linda Style
Texas Hold 'Em
Jake Chandler swore he'd never return to River Bluff, Texas, after being run out of town when he was eighteen, wrongfully accused of arson. But a funeral brings him back. And Rachel Diamonte, the witness to his supposed crime, just might be the woman who keeps him here. Because when it comes to love, the stakes are high....

#1459 LOOKING FOR SOPHIE • Roz Denny Fox
Garnet Patton's life hasn't been the same since her ex-husband abducted their five-year-old daughter and left Alaska. Then Julian Cavanaugh, a detective from Atlanta, comes to town, claiming he might have some new information. Will he be able to find her daughter...and will he be able to lead Garnet back to love?

#1460 BABY MAKES THREE • Molly O'Keefe
The Mitchells of Riverview Inn
Asking for his ex-wife's help is the last thing Gabe Mitchell wants to do. But he needs a chef, and Alice is the best. Working together proves their attraction is still strong. So is the issue that drove them apart. Is this their second chance...or will infertility destroy them again?

#1461 STRANGER IN A SMALL TOWN • Margaret Watson
A Little Secret
Kat is determined to adopt Regan, her best friend's child. Only one thing stands in her way—Seth Anderson. Seth has just learned he is Regan's father, and even though he's no family man, he wants to do right by the little girl. Especially once he realizes Kat is a suspect in the investigation he's conducting.

#1462 ONE MAN TO PROTECT THEM • Suzanne Cox
He says he can protect her and the children, but how can Jayden Miller possibly trust Luke Taylor—when the public defender is clearly working for some very nasty men? With no one else in Cypress Landing to turn to, Jayden is forced to put their lives in his hands....

#1463 DOCTOR IN HER HOUSE • Amy Knupp
When Katie Salinger came back to recuperate from her latest extreme-sport adventure, she didn't expect her dad to have her childhood home up for sale. The memories tied to it are all she has left of her mom. Worse: there's an offer...from the mysterious Dr. Noah Fletcher.

HSRCNM1107